LAWLESS

SOSA & G BOOK ONE

MERCY B

CONTENTS

STAY IN THE KNOW

TEXT **MERCYB** TO 555888 TO SIGN UP FOR
UPDATES, SPOILERS, GIVEAWAYS,
ANNOUNCEMENTS & ANY NEW MERCY B
PUBLICATIONS RELEASES.

To any and everyone who has been a part of my writing journey, I'm blessed by your generosity.

PROLOGUE

I STOOD SIX FEET SIX, nearly touching the roof inside the safe that I'd buried inside of my basement. The construction on the addition to my home had cost me over $50,000, but I wasn't complaining. The ceiling-to-floor steel cage held my life's valuable possessions. Looking to my left, right, and then over my shoulder, I felt an overwhelming sense of pride, much like a father who'd raised his children in the admonition of the Lord, and they'd gone off to make him a proud papa.

Each bill that I'd struggled and strived to get felt like a child that I'd bore. Within the many years that I was in the game, I'd birthed millions of them—twelve and a possible to be exact. I gawked at the neatly arranged bills, ammunition, gold, and jewelry that littered the space. I'd always had a thing about banks.

For more reasons than one, I never trusted them. For

that, not even one of my hard-earned dollars had been handed over to them for safekeeping. I felt that no one could better protect my fortune than I could. Besides, I'd have a lot of explaining to do when the government asked questions concerning my funds. Those were questions I'd never have the answer to.

"It's been a long time coming." I cracked a smile. Reaching behind my ear, I grabbed the pre-rolled gold foil and lit it with the lighter that I'd been holding in my hand. "A long motherfucking time." I inhaled, nodding my head as I spoke.

The smoke filled my lungs as I pulled once more. Today wasn't just any day for me. It was just as monumental as the day I'd placed my hand on my first brick. Over fifteen years of hustling had gotten me to the place I was today, standing in the midst of twelve million dollars with a blunt to my lips.

"And a nigga wouldn't change a thing." I exhaled.

A few more pulls, and I started to feel the effects of the orange kush that I'd rolled just an hour prior. My eyes became heavy as I stared down at the navy-blue duffle bag that I'd brought along with me. Bending down with the blunt still hanging from my lips, I unzipped the duffle and pulled it up by the handles.

The emptiness caused it to be light in weight, but the minute I began pulling stacks of money from my piles of cash, that changed. Stack after stack, I piled money into the huge duffle, stopping only to pull on my blunt a bit more. As I placed the stacks into the bag, I kept count in my head. I didn't want to run the risk of giving away a penny more than I should of my hard-earned money.

"That about does it." I finished off my blunt and threw it beside my feet.

Lifting up, I smashed the remainder of it with my size eleven Dirty Bred 13 Jordan sneakers. Turning on my heels, I shut off the lights to the safe and stepped outside of it. Reaching across my chest, I pulled the silver door closed before placing my hand on the pad beside it, locking the safe back. Once the light transformed from orange to green, I knew that I was in the clear.

Climbing the single set of stairs, I ended up on the actual basement level floor. Once my electronics and La-Z-Boy were in plain view, I reached behind me and slid the heavy door to the right. I tossed my bag onto the floor before pulling the ancient rug over the small indention that the lower basement door created. Soon after, I pulled the entertainment set back over the rug. Once all was well, I grabbed my duffle bag, along with the one that I'd placed at the basement door the previous day, and headed up to the first level of my home.

Checking my watch, I realized that I had nearly ten minutes to spare before it was go time. With that, I placed the bags at my back door before hiking up the stairs two by two. My long legs helped me to reach my bedroom much faster than the average. It only took seconds for me to lay eyes on my sleeping damsel.

Sprawled out, twisted inside of our covers, Millie slept; I couldn't help but admire my very own sleeping beauty. It had probably taken nearly the entire night for her to find comfort, and though I hated to wake her, I felt as if I had no choice. Had I departed without a word, my beauty would quickly become a beast. To save face, I took the initiative.

Chuckling, I positioned myself at the edge of our bed, just before her. Examining Millie from top to bottom, I was tickled by her chosen stance for the night. Two fluffy pillows were placed between her legs and one under her back. The other one was underneath her long tresses. Had I been lying beside her, I would've been assed out, but that didn't matter. All that mattered was her comfort.

"Mi," I called softly, acknowledging the pet name that I'd given her years prior. Reaching out, I placed my large hand on her growing belly. At six months, she was glowing in every sense of the word. I thought that she was beautiful before, but the pregnancy had given her a more somber-like beauty.

"Millie," I leaned down and whispered in her ear.

She was usually a light sleeper, but times had been hard for her lately. With her bulging belly, it took hours for her to get comfortable enough to sleep the night away. Some nights were nearly impossible to rest. Our daughter was forever causing trouble.

However, Millie never complained a bit. She was happy in pregnancy and rolled with whatever punches

4

our unborn child threw our way. In fact, she was fascinated by the changes her body was quickly adapting to. She was hopeful that she'd soon figure out how to rest easily. For now, she did what she could.

"Yes... baby," Millie whined. She nearly wanted to cry. The crackling of her voice tugged at my heartstrings, ones that were solely attached to her and the being that would be birthed in a few short months.

Sleep had just overcome her, and I was waking her already. "I hate to wake you, but it's time for me to go." I rubbed her stomach in circular motions. The feeling was so soothing that it was coaching Millie right back into the slumber she'd been in. This wasn't helping much in my situation.

"You hear me, Mi?" I questioned, removing my hand from her stomach.

"Yes... baby," she repeated.

"Open your eyes."

Utterly helpless in the situation, I was tempted to let her be. But I knew that I'd be even more heavy-hearted if she wound up disappointed in my sudden departure. I wouldn't hear or feel the end of her wrath for weeks. As mellow as baby girl was, she had a fierce mean streak that I steered clear of at all costs, even if that meant waking her after finally finding comfort to rest.

"I can't." Millie groaned, a single tear falling from her right eye though she'd never opened it.

I was regretting even coming up to bother her, but I

didn't want to hear the bickering later, so I did what I thought necessary. "I ain't mean to wake you. Rest well, love. I'm out." I stood from the bed.

With her eyes still closed, she replied, "I'm sorry. I'm just tired." Her whimpers were like daggers through my chest.

"I understand." Leaning back down, I kissed her forehead before kissing her lips. She was still with me. I could sense her appreciation as she puckered her lips for a second kiss. I obliged before hearing a heavy sigh emerge from her throat. It was necessary that I let her be, so I did. Lifting, again, I cleared my throat and straightened my posture.

"Come back to me," she recited her favorite line whenever I went into the streets to handle my business.

"Where else I'm gone go?" I smiled. It may have been corny as shit, but it was our shit. We refused to expunge of each other's presence without saying it.

Gazing at my wife, I knew that I was making the right decision. While the option was still on the table, I wanted to take advantage. Soon, my daughter would be born, and life as we knew it would never be the same.

"Nowhere," she finalized.

"As long as you know." With that, I gathered myself and headed for the stairs. It took every ounce of strength not to climb in the bed and coax Millie back to sleep before joining her.

"YOU SURE ABOUT THIS SHIT?" Cayman asked the minute he planted his ass in the passenger seat.

I had come to scoop him just as always. We were due to make a drop in less than an hour. For me, it was my final payment to the commander in chief. I was done. My ship had sailed, and shit had come to the crossroads for me. There was a point in life when I'd rather be nowhere other than the streets, but shit was different now.

The game had changed drastically, and loyal motherfuckers were few and far apart. I couldn't trust half the niggas on my team as far as I could throw them. On the other hand, niggas were making reckless decisions and getting popped left and right. As if that wasn't enough, they were turning informant overnight. The first chance they got, they were singing like the bitches in the operas on Broadway.

I wanted no parts in the foolishness and decided that my departure was inevitable. If I didn't remove myself from the game, either the law or my enemies would. Refusing to give either the satisfaction, I opted to leave myself. Now was a better time than ever.

"I'm positive. I've never been so sure about shit else in my life."

"Well, shit... I'm with you no matter what. I appreciate you handing over your land and shit. I got a whole team of heavy hitters waiting to expand. This shit was right on time. I can't lie though. A nigga gon' miss getting this money with you."

Cayman and I had been boys since shitty diapers and rubber duck baths. Our mothers had been the best of friends, and we fell right in line. Neither of us was anymore planted in the game than the other. In so many ways, we were on the same level. However, I was more of the brains, and Cayman was the mad machine. He'd let his choppa speak before him any day.

We were like night and day though, down to the appearance. I was as black as tar. The only thing light about me was the white around my eyes and my pearly teeth. If it weren't for the two, you wouldn't be able to distinguish me from the dark of the night.

Cayman stood just as tall as me. However, he was caramel in skin complexion. He wore a low cut as well, but his curls peeked out from the top of his dome. He was a pretty nigga, and motherfuckers were always mistaken by the fact. They thought that he was a pussy half of the time until he was hot on their trail or emptying his clip into their thick skull. Whereas Cayman would forever be a ladies' man, I had put my player ways on the back burner when I'd set my sights on Millie's fine ass. Immediately, I was smitten, and our thing blossomed like wildfire. Neither of us could control that shit if we wanted to.

"Same shit I was thinking. For old time's sake..." I pulled another blunt from behind my ear. I stayed laced. You wouldn't catch me dead without a pre-rolled blunt of the stickiest shit around the land.

Looking at his Rolex timepiece, compliments of me

for his twenty-ninth birthday, Cayman saw that they had another thirty minutes before their drop-off was scheduled. We were always the first to make it on the scene. On both of our ends, we felt it necessary to case out the scene. It didn't matter how many years we'd been doing this shit; we never got too comfortable, knowing that comfort could lead to our demise.

"Forever on your toes," was what we'd always say about being careful and notable of your surroundings at all times.

"For old times sake..." Cayman reached into his pocket and handed me the lighter that he had on him.

Just as I blazed, Cayman's cell phone rang. He frowned upon noticing that a restricted caller was attempting to reach him

"Watch out!" was all we heard through his speaker before the windows to my hummer shattered, and bullets rained through.

I dropped the blunt that was hanging from my mouth as the sound of the windows startled me. Before I could take cover, I felt myself losing consciousness. A burning sensation ripped through my body as I closed my eyes but not before the crimson blood leaked through my solid white tee.

"We out!" the assaulters yelled. Their deed had been done.

Gripping my pistol, it felt miles away even with it being curled up in my hand. My index finger released the trigger that it held hostage as I sighed and began rubbing the soreness from my eyes. The darkness paired with the softness that surrounded me assured me that I was home, in my bed, dreaming—again. At least once a week, the same dream haunted me in my sleep, and I'd considered it the warning before destruction. Not one to take threats to my freedom and safety lightly, I'd began planning for the unforeseeable future. Whatever was headed my way, I was ready for.

With my homie at my waist, I slid from the bed and dragged him into the kitchen. I ate with my piece, slept with my piece, and showered with my piece. There wasn't a place I'd visit that she wasn't permitted. We were an item, and one wouldn't make its presence without the company of the other. It had been this way for years.

Descending my steps, I sluggishly entered my kitchen after taking them two by two. The lone glass in the center of the counter had been placed for this partic-ular reason—a late-night sip. The coldness from the surface was due to the air conditioner that automati-cally cooled my home's temperature to an even sixty-six degrees. A button or two were pressed to inform my fridge that I'd be needing both crushed ice and water to remove the clumps from my throat that had formed during the recurring dream.

While others considered nightmares to be full of demons and other theological shit that none of us quite understood, my fears being played out before my eyes each night was what I considered a nightmare. The fear of my life or my freedom being snatched away had me thinking differently, moving differently, and feeling differently. I hadn't been the same man since after the second night it came to visit me in my sleep. The blindfold I'd had over my eyes was removed, and I was seeing so much clearer now.

ONE

GAUGE

I couldn't decide on which dress I'd be wearing on my date. On the one hand, I preferred the little black dress, but it completely covered my assets. And to be frank, I wanted to flaunt every God-given curve that I'd been blessed with. On the other hand, the cut of the burgundy bodycon dress made me feel heavenly, but I didn't want to overdress for the occasion. As of yet, I wasn't sure where he'd be taking me.

Unlike the three I'd entertained prior, I actually admired this candidate. He was more my speed, working class, youthful, conscious, and overly hand-some. Twenty-four hours before he'd requested my number in the fresh soup section of Central Market, I'd sworn off men and dating all in the same sentence.

Brielle, my best friend since kindergarten, and I were having the dark discussion on the state of our men in this day, and neither of us was satisfied with our conclusions. I'd been enjoying the benefits of being single for far too long and was ready to entertain someone other than myself.

Brielle, unfortunately, had been on the receiving end of fresh bruises marked by the pain of her boyfriend, Marlo's, infidelity. They'd been together for three years, yet he had yet to digest the fact that he was no longer a single man or wasn't apart of a poly situation.

And I felt for her, which was why I hesitated on starting up a new group chat that included her new cell number. The last thing I wanted to do was shove my plans for the night into her face, knowing that her scars were still bleeding. She was still trying to adjust, knowing that the love of her life happened to be someone besides the man that she'd catered to physically, mentally and emotionally in the last few years.

I'm sure she'll understand, I reasoned with myself. I'd redressed far too many times not to seek a second and third opinion. With her agony weighing heavy on my heart, I tried remembering the final four digits of her cell number while adding her to a new group that would also include our friend Sauni.

Ladies. He's taking me to dinner. First date blues.

Quick question. Which one?

Black or Burgundy?

Before submitting the message, I attached a photo of myself in each dress with them side by side for comparison. I could always count on Brielle's bluntness and Sauni's subtleness. Together, they would finalize my decision.

Three minutes later, and I was still staring at my cell, wondering what either of them was preoccupied with that they couldn't respond to my message. With Brielle having a new number and screening each call that came through, I'd expected her to be the first to respond.

Hello? Brielle. Sauni.

I needed them to understand the urgency of the situation. In less than twenty minutes, Tyler would be outside. The last thing I wanted was to keep him waiting.

Sauni: Sorry Buttercup, I had my hands full. Which do you like most? I'd like to base my opinion off that because they're both amazing. I can't exactly choose, either.

As I began to construct a message to Sauni, Brielle finally decided to join the party. Sighing, I erased the tad bit that I'd written, knowing she'd be the voice of reasoning. My eyes scanned her message as embarrassment flushed my cheeks.

Unknown: My name isn't Brielle and neither is it Sauni, but if I had to choose then I would go with the burgundy jawn. As

15

a man, I'd be thoroughly impressed if my date was coming like that. But then again, you're not my date, so the black one feels more suitable.

"Oh shit," I chastised myself, quickly exiting the short thread and accessing my recent calls. I'd replaced the final one in Brielle's cell number with a seven. Returning to the group that I'd created, I began typing a new message, but Sauni had beaten me to the point.

Sauni: I'm assuming you're single.

Unknown: Depends on who's asking.

Sauni: I'm asking for my friend... Who is single.

Unknown: Then, yeah.

I watched the fuckery for as long as I could before interfering, having no interest in entertaining a stranger who I'd happened to misdial by accident.

Please, accept my apology. I didn't mean to add you to the group.

I responded before deleting the thread and beginning a fresh one. This time, I was sure to save Brielle's new number before sending the same photo and question. As expected, Brielle responded to the message right away.

Brielle: Burgundy, bitch.

It would've pained her to send a simple reply. While I was a mixture between bold and bashful, Brielle was the ultimate mouthpiece. Sauni was the quieter one of the bunch, which meant there was the perfect balance between us three.

Brielle. I warned her.

Sauni: That's the one I think she should wear, too.

I wondered where Sauni had disappeared to that suddenly. As a notification pinged, alerting me of two new messages in the group that had been erased, I was quickly informed about her prior whereabouts. She was too busy keeping the other group up and running instead of sharing her opinion in the correct one.

With curiosity clouding my judgment, I returned to the messages to see what had been said in my absence and wished I'd just minded my business once inside. Sauni was up to no good, and the young man she was conversing with wasn't either.

Sauni: Well, she's sent a photo, so I think it is only right that you do the same.

Unknown: Only because I want to be the nigga she calls if shit don't work out with ole boy tonight.

Attached to his last message was one of him covered in red. Denim shirt and shoes were all deep shades of red that complimented his brown skin. While he wasn't necessarily the darkest I'd ever dated, he was definitely in second place. I'd have to give credit to Omi, the first-place winner, because he was undeniably African and exposed to unfathomable rays of sunlight every day as a child.

Whoever this gentleman was, he had the most heavenly features, large, round eyes, a wide nose, and lips that were too perfect in dimension. That smile of his was torturous as he posed for the camera, hand caught in the hairs of his thick beard. If I had to put a number on it, I'd say that he was between the ages of twenty-six and twenty-eight, but none of that mattered. I had a date to prepare for. Besides, he seemed like the type to have a plethora of women riding his bone, and I refused to be just another contact in his book.

Sauni: Brielle, I'm adding you to the other group she made. You must see this man whose number she mistakenly dialed.

Brielle: Put me in the game, coach.

I couldn't stand those two, especially not now. Instead of responding to either group, I muted the notifications from both and continued preparing myself for the night ahead. Of course, whoever the man was in our messages was handsome, but he wasn't necessarily my type.

The type with a legit nine-to-five and a 401-k in place. The tattoos that littered his body assured me that he hadn't gotten hired anywhere in corporate America. It was hard enough as a young, tactful black woman to secure a spot on someone's clock.

The chances of him gaining employment were laughable.

Because I'd be wearing the burgundy dress, I grabbed my black booties and black studded clutch. The two complimented each other well, in addition to my dress. Within ten minutes, I was fully dressed and spritzing my body with perfume my father had gotten me for my birthday this year—Flowerbomb, which had quickly become my favorite fragrance.

Five minutes prior to our scheduled pick-up time, I unraveled the spirals that I had rolled my hair with. At the sound of my alarm, I fluffed my hair to my liking and was ready to walk out of the door. The issue was no one was outside. I'd been peeking out of the window for the past three minutes to be sure that I wouldn't keep Tyler waiting.

Women were known procrastinators, but fortunately, I didn't fall into that category. Very punctual, I couldn't remember a single event or engagement I'd attended and was late to unless it was completely out of my control and due to others. But personally, I was a stickler for time, knowing that every second could be useful.

Five minutes elapsed before I began contemplating the dreaded, "Where are you?" call. The thought that not everyone was as punctual as me weighed heavy on my mind like a ton of bricks, so I rested my limbs on the couch and decided to wait at least another ten minutes before calling. Ten minutes turned into twenty when the urge to reach out overcame me. With my cell already in my hand, I called the number associated with his contact and waited to hear his voice.

Instead, I received his voicemail. "The person you are trying to reach has a voice mailbox that hasn't been set up. Please hang up and try your call again later."

Sighing deeply, I tried finding comfort on the couch without the risk of ruining my curls before conjuring a decent text message. The certainty of our pending union didn't dwindle as I pecked my perfectly manicured nails across my phone.

I had been preparing to go on this date for at least twenty-four hours with Tyler reiterating the fact that he couldn't wait to see me again. I'd refused any form of physical contact unless we commenced with a date. During the Netflix and Chill era that we were currently in, I was desperate to set myself apart from the rest.

Tyler was agreeable with my revelation, or at least I considered him to be. That was until I realized I'd called him three times in the last thirty minutes, and he hadn't answered a single call. In fact, it seemed as if I'd been placed on his blocked list by the repetitive voice of the woman on nearly everyone's voicemail I'd encountered over the last few years.

"Shit." Frustration was apparent as I tossed my cell toward the other end of the couch.

Suddenly, ruining my curls wasn't as devastating of a thought as it had been afore the shame of being stood up overpowered me. As it seemed, I couldn't win for losing. This entire dating realm was a pile of bullshit that I had been stepping foot in since I decided to reenter.

I could feel the folds of my face scrunching and disfiguring as I thought back to our conversations and tried processing the fact that it was all smoke that had quickly blown over. While I considered Tyler to be above the handful of maniacs that I had encountered in the last few months, I'd like to go on the record by saying that neither of them was a coward. They hadn't stood me up or discontinued my calls.

Instead of blaming myself for his immaturity, I allowed the muscles of my face to relax along with my speeding heart rate. There was no point in drowning in sorrows that weren't rooted within me. It was Tyler who seemed to have lost his damned mind. As I began to unwind, exhaustion swooned me. I hadn't taken the time to consider how cluttered it was with tasks that required both my mental and physical competence.

Absentmindedly, I found myself falling into a light slumber that I was unaware of until my cell phone began chiming. The slob running down the right side of my mouth assured me that I'd needed the quickie. Only in instances I woke with saliva on my pillow were when the day had beaten the crap out of me. This one was no exception.

"Shit," I fussed, fumbling with the decorative pillows on the couch to find my cell.

Strangely, I felt it in my heart that Tyler had come to grips with his foolishness and was calling to apologize. More than likely, he'd attempt to schedule another date, but I wasn't giving him a second chance to stand me up. That shit was history.

Upon retrieving my cell, I noticed the unknown number while simultaneously furrowing my brows. "Why is this man texting me?" I questioned.

The time displayed on my phone informed me that I'd been asleep for two hours. It had only seemed like a few minutes, but the best naps always did. It was after ten, which really had me questioning his timing.

TWO

GAUGE

Unknown: Your friends are checking for you in the lil group shit you put me in.

What do they want? The other conversations were muted, so the notifications weren't coming through. I could imagine what was being said about me amongst those two.

Unknown: To know how your date went.

I got stood up. There was no need to dwell on the situation. He could relay the message, and I'd follow up with my girls in the morning. I wanted to return to my bedroom and prepare for bed.

There was a lengthy pause, the gray bubble appearing and then disappearing. Unknowingly, I'd held my breath until his message came through. I considered shutting down the entire thread between us, but the rejection I had received earlier caused his attention to be a bit more appealing.

Unknown: You still dressed?

Yeah. Shit, what more did I have to lose? My pride had already been bruised enough for the night.

Unknown: Share ya location. I'm on my way.

Share my location? I don't even know you. He couldn't have been serious. I mean, he was a complete stranger that I'd misdialed. Wanting my location was a bit intrusive.

Unknown: Did you know the mother-fucker that stood you up, tonight?

No. Well, he had a point. I hadn't known Tyler long, possibly four days, give or take a few hours.

Unknown: Location, then.

Where are we going? Since he was demanding answers, I needed some of my own. In addition to sharing my location, I requested it.

Unknown: You'll see when we get there. Rude. The arrogance attached to street niggas was sexy as shit, but I begged to differ tonight. Tonight, I needed straight answers.

There isn't much open this late. Maybe we can reschedule.

Hello? His responses had discontinued. No gray bubble. Nothing.

Can I at least have your name? I tried a gentler approach to get him talking again.

Unknown: Sosa. Damn. Sosa.

Sosa, where are you taking me?

I waited inevitably for a response that would never come. Upon realizing this, I scurried to our group message in order to review the photo he'd sent. My friends had a slew of messages within the thread that made me groan in agony. I could only imagine how frustrated he was with the constant notifications.

"Sosa." I repeated.

In all honesty, I loved the name. It was becoming of him. The deep, dark-brown skin, rugged yet splendid appearance, and the overall bad-boy demeanor he possessed was all conclusive in his simple and unique title. He looked like a Sosa, or to me at least.

Immediately, I exited the messages and accessed my social media folder. Instagram was the first to receive my attention. I typed his name in variations to see if I'd stumble across his account, but I came up empty-handed. The same was for Facebook, Snapchat, and Twitter as well.

I chalked it up to him being a bit clever with his user ID and made a mental note to ask him about his social media handles before the night ended. It wasn't that I cared to keep up with him. It was simply because I wanted to know all that I could about him. Social media said a lot about people these days, whether true or false.

Time had gotten away from me as I attempted to investigate this intriguing being. The knock on my door startled me and brought me back to reality. Suddenly, nerves that my body had been absent of began sprouting and causing for clammy hands. Sure not to ruin my dress, I opted to wipe my sweaty palms on the end of my couch before checking myself out in the mirror. There was a second knock, prompting me to lose the bashfulness I'd encountered in the last few seconds and not keep him waiting any longer.

Goddamn. I nearly closed the door in his face. A man this fine was nothing but trouble. Quickly, I came to the conclusion that red must've been his favorite color because he was draped in it tonight as well. And the fit that he wore before me wasn't in resemblance to the one in the photo he had sent. I'd studied it like an exam the night before testing.

"You chose burgundy, huh?"

The fact that he was standing on my porch instead of honking the horn or texting me to let me know that he was outside spoke volumes. I'd heard what Sosa had said, but the immense pressure I felt in his presence kept me quiet and staring back with the possibility of looking like a damn fool. Smitten, my sight trailed from the top of his head to the soles of his feet.

Sosa was wearing a red V-neck, simple as hell, but he made it look three times as exclusive. He'd probably gotten it from the corner market in the hood, but one would think it came straight from the runway. His denim didn't hug his ass, neither did they sag. The belt around his waist wasn't for show but was actually doing its job by maintaining the weight of his pants and keeping them from falling.

The red designer sneakers stretched for quite a bit, causing me to wonder if he was a member of the hood wood tribe—a tribe that my friends and I had made up full of men from the hood who were slanging serious wood. Jewelry clung to his body—neck, both wrists, one ear, and his teeth—lighting the darkness that consumed us. I was a lengthy girl, standing a proud five feet seven without heels, yet this nigga seemed to have an entire foot on me. In my heels, I was barely shoulder length.

"You finished?"

"Excuse me?"

"Your examination," he replied, feet gapped and legs spread. *He was definitely a part of the hood wood tribe.* My mind was completely in the gutter.

"I'm sorry." Panic stricken, I stepped onto the porch and turned to lock the door. "So rude of me."

His silence was vexatious. I hardly wanted to return to him because I was sure he was checking me out now. Double standard, I know. It was completely okay for me to fuck him with my eyes, but I was haunted at the thought of him doing the same. I'd have to get better at that, but tonight wouldn't be the night.

"Uh." Of course, his eyes were wandering.

"Listen."

Sosa stepped forward and had no intentions of halting until my back was against my front door, and his body was pressed up against mine. In no way did I feel threatened, which was highly unlikely for me. As an assault survivor, I was leery about men and their closeness. It always rubbed me the wrong way and caused anxiety to rise in my chest.

My breath somehow got lodged in my throat after inhaling his intoxicating scent. While I'd expected to smell something delectable on his frame, I was addressed by the boisterous scent of marijuana and jolly rancher. His stained blue tongue that I watched with intent as he spoke was evidence that he'd been eating jolly ranchers to remove the fogginess and funkiness from his breath that weed tended to leave behind.

"Before we leave this porch, I need you to drop that shy shit. I'm just some ole hood nigga. Ain't shit to be conflicted, confused, or questioned. I'm just here to make your night right after a fuck nigga nearly sent you to bed with a frown. No pressure. No expectations."

Sighing, I nodded in understanding. Thankfully, he eased back a bit, giving me the space to process the limp dick that I'd felt on my leg. That thing was the size of one of the healthy cucumbers that I preferred from the grocery store. Imagining it erect was too much for my little mind to digest, so I didn't.

"You look beautiful by the way."

"I like your teeth," I retorted before closing my eyes and chastising myself. That was...

"So fucking lame, baby girl. But I like that," he completed my thought.

"Where... Where are we going?"

"Nothing has changed. You'll see when we get there."

Underneath the porchlight, I could see the haze in his eyes. They were low enough to connect with one another, which made me wonder how he could even see—or function. Concluding his statement, he smiled and nearly sent me into cardiac arrest. His fangs were covered in diamonds, while the rest of his pearly white teeth were only outlined with silver; platinum seemed more suiting for a man of his caliber.

"Open faces," he spoke, extending his arm and insisting that I lead the way.

"Pardon me?"

"My teeth. They're called open faces."

He was behind me, keeping a short distance as I walked down the small path that led from my home into my driveway. I was renting a two-bedroom home simply because it was cheaper than any apartment that I had applied for three years ago while a sophomore in college. It was apparent that the campus life didn't agree with me, but I didn't want to break myself by trying to afford housing. Instead, I chose rent that my refund check would cover at least three-fourths of and paid the remainder with my checks from work every month.

I assumed he wasn't paying much attention to my

feet, because his eyes were occupied with my ass, and Sosa ran into the back of me after I'd stopped mid-stride. Confusion was evident on my face as I turned around to question his logic. The outdated Honda Accord sitting in my driveway couldn't have belonged to the man that was just standing on my porch. Even in the photo he had sent, there was a large B on the grill of the car he was standing in front of.

I prayed this wasn't a situation where a young man was flaunting shit that wasn't his own. It was the last thing I wanted to confront or had the time to deal with. I wasn't opposed to dating middle-class men, but lower-class was pushing the perimeter. Personally, I was a decent enough woman in decent standing and could afford to choose whom I gave my time to.

"Sosa, is it?"

He didn't answer. Instead, he stood off to the side, wondering what my next few words would entail. His wait wasn't enduring or in vain, because I spat them out swiftly.

"Is this the car that will take us to the real car?" I had to know. "Because—"

"What's your name, baby girl? I never got it."

The thought hadn't crossed my mind. He hadn't taken my name. "Gauge," I replied, shifting my weight and becoming frustrated.

"Gauge. I can fuck with that." He nodded.

"I asked a question," firmly, I stated, not caring for the delay I was receiving.

"And I plan to give you an answer when I'm ready." He emphasized by shrugging.

The stare-off commenced, me not budging and him not giving a flying shit about my sudden displeasure. It felt as if an eternity had elapsed before his lips parted, and his baritone reached my eardrums.

"I'm that nigga whether I'm in a Bentley or a bucket," he confirmed my suspicions. I was immediately relieved that I hadn't overestimated his financial status because I would've been pissed at myself. I'd always been good at these types of things.

"Flossing isn't the only evidence of wealth, G."

G? I wanted to correct him, but the letter sounded so good rolling from his lips that I simply rolled with it. Without a response, I twirled on my heels and continued. He was right. Once I'd reached the car, I extended my hand to open the door but was startled by his warning.

"Nothing will get you sent back in the house to think about your actions quicker than trying to put me out of a job. If I can't at least open your door, then what am I good for?"

"You don't have to—"

"My mother has turned over in her grave over enough shit I've done. I'm sure she's trying to rest right now. My wish isn't to disturb her tonight." Sosa leaned forward and opened the door to the car and watched me slide in. "You good?" he questioned, standing outside of the car and looking down at me.

31

"I'm sorry," sympathetically, I responded with a saddened look displayed across my face.

"For what?"

"Your mother."

"Shit. I'm sure the dirt treating her better than this shitty as world ever could."

With that, he slammed the door and walked around to the driver's side. I expected us to pull off immediately, but we continued to wait outside of my house after he'd started the engine of the car. At the sight of him slicing the gold foiled wrap with a small box cutter, I knew why the wait was necessary. He needed to roll himself another blunt.

The thought of my hair smelling like a pound of weed occurred, and I wanted to scream. I'd just shampooed my hair and wouldn't be needing another shampoo for at least a week under normal circumstances. However, with Mr. Sosa firing up in a few, the task would need to be tackled the following day.

"G," he started. "I'm about to tell you some shit that'll probably upset you, but you'll be aight."

"Should I ask for you to tell me what it is, or are you..."

"I'm going to tell you anyway." He tapped the grinder and distributed the orange hybrid marijuana buds across the paper.

"Figures."

"Where we're headed, you may want to slip on

something more comfortable. I don't have fancy reservations or nothing like that. I'm just winging it."

"What?" I heard him, but I was being sure that I'd heard him correctly.

"Go change, G." He placed the blunt to his mouth. "Throw on some jeans or something. Shit, I don't know."

"You didn't think it would've been appropriate to tell me this before you pulled up or even when I stepped out of my door?"

"I'm a man, baby girl. A selfish one if I must admit. I wanted to see you in that dress."

"And after you saw me in it?" I asked, completely shocked at his revelation and reasoning.

"I wanted to see you from behind." Shaking his head, he chuckled at his own fuckery. "You locked your door too quick. This is your fault."

"My fault?" I screeched. "Just like a nigga."

"G, I'm going to be out here. Put on your favorite pair of jeans and a nice little top or something." I'd only been in his presence for minutes, and the nonchalant attitude that he possessed was pissing me off and arousing me at the same time.

Had this been anyone else, I would've returned to my home and not came back out. But I found myself locking my door for the second time within ten minutes of reentering my home. When I rested my ass in the seat, I noticed Sosa was rolling a second blunt with the first one still at his lips.

"Better?"

"Perfect." He nodded, putting the unfinished blunt down and continuing to pull off the one he'd been smoking. "Here." Sosa handed me the aux cord. "Put something on that you like. I'm certain my music won't entertain you."

THREE

SOSA

She was kicking my ass, but I couldn't admit to caring. In fact, I didn't. Even with my competitiveness, I allowed her to take the lead and talk her shit simply because I enjoyed it and wanted to see her smile. Given I didn't know this girl from a can of paint, I wasn't doing shit, and my nights usually only consisted of an old film and counting paper.

My thoughts wouldn't dispose of her after I'd seen her thick ass thighs and beautiful face in the picture she'd mistakenly sent me. Again, I wasn't acquainted with this woman, but the thought of her entertaining another nigga while looking that damn good etched away at me. I'd put her to the back of my thoughts after the bizarre incident, but her friends kept my thoughts alive by continuing to vouch for their friend and bringing me even more entertainment in the form of photos, videos, and accolades of hers. Not to mention the fact that they referred to her as Mili.

Though spelled differently and obviously wasn't Gauge's name, I was reminded of the dreams I'd been having of the beautiful woman lying across my bed that I referred to as my wife. In this game, there were a few things that I avoided—Cops, robbers, and women. Of course, I had my fun with the bitches that swung my way, but I could honestly say that I'd never even gone as far as taking a woman on a date.

In my line of work, they weren't to be trusted. I'd seen the most down bitches fold at the sight of trouble. The thought of doing a day in jail after maxing out bank accounts, buying the latest fashions, flying out on a minute's notice, sitting courtside at games, making sure everyone knew that they were fucking a nigga with money had them bitches singing like the birds they were. It wasn't a risk I'd been willing to take—still wasn't.

That's exactly why I would punish the pussy after I let her beat my ass in bowling and bounce. No hard feelings, just hard dick that would make up for the asshole she'd gotten stood up by earlier. As I watched her bend over in the hip-hugging jeans and roll the ball, I silently thanked ole boy, whoever the fuck it was and wherever the fuck he was at.

"I don't hear much of that smart-ass mouth of yours now," she boasted, swearing she was doing something.

If only she knew that I could kick her ass with my

eyes closed, she wouldn't be so confident. Her skills weren't even mediocre. She was trash. But women seemed most fun when they felt as if they had the upper hand, so I'd let her have that. As well, the nachos, snacks, and candy that I'd been consuming were soothing the massive hunger I possessed due to the munchies.

"Can't win 'em all." I stood and waited for the ball I preferred to come up. Someone from another lane and I were sharing it.

"Ayo, Sosa," I heard from behind.

I whipped around to find my right-hand, Cayman, headed in my direction. Dismissing the thought of the ball, I posted as he made his way over. It was no surprise in running into him. Cayman and I were polar. While he was the life of the party, I was the owner of the club the party was being thrown in who never left his office or fraternized with the partygoers. That had never been my thing.

"Nigga, I didn't know you could stay out past curfew. It's what? Eleven? And you out here enjoying life. That shit is unheard of."

"Well, listen closer, nigga." I shrugged.

"What's good? What you got on the board?" Taking a peek at the scores, he found even more humor in my presence. "And you losing."

"By choice," I assured him. "What's good?"

There were twenty-four hours in a day, and Cayman fucked around at least twenty of them. The other four, he was sleep. A comedian, clown, all of that could be used to describe him. Again, polar. Though I loved him, I was nothing like this nigga. We'd known each other since jits and were willing to ride for one another until the caskets dropped.

While niggas called motherfuckers their friends just off their presence in their life, my list was simple. Plus one, and I was done. My definition of friend was a bit different from others, and my requirements were a bit extensive. To be frank, associates weren't even my jam. Too many niggas equaled too many feelings. Too many feelings had never brought in too many figures for me. I'd gotten to where I was without obtaining them and had no plans of obtaining them before my casket dropped.

Others measured friendship through time and cooperation. As for me, friendship was established the minute shit got ugly, or one was caught in a jam. How the motherfuckers you called your friends reacted was what set them apart from the rest. Cayman had been in the trenches with me, getting his hands dirty and never folding under pressure. He kept a shotty on him and was always itching to use it.

"Shit. Ayo, who is ole girl with your girl?"

"My girl." I felt the crinkling of the skin on my face.

"Nigga, you ain't never brought a bitch a can of soda, and you out here tricking at the bowling alley where all the birds and wannabe ballers hang. You ain't trying to be low-key. Ya more laxed than I've ever seen you. Shit, I think the frown lines around ya mouth done even disappeared a bit. Don't front, nigga. Like I said. Who is ole girl with your girl?"

"You've been the type to talk a whole bunch of shit without saying nothing." I turned to find Gauge engaged in a conversation with a dark-skinned chick that was nearly the same size as her, only she was thicker with bolder features and lips too damned big for her face.

While her body was something to see, she could use a few surgical procedures to acquire a face to match. She wasn't necessarily ugly, but she definitely wasn't the cutest thing either. Or, maybe it was because she was standing beside Gauge, who was insanely beautiful, which downplayed ole girl.

Gauge was brown, like the paper bags I used to carry my dope in as a jit but not as dark. Her hair was big as shit, but I wouldn't consider it a fro. Just a bunch of curls, which were blonde in color. I could imagine her putting those harsh chemicals in it to obtain the color she had.

As well, I could conclude that she had something mixed with the melanin in her skin, possibly white, possibly Italian—one or the other, and I'd bet my last on it. The silkiness of her hair, softness of her skin, and the speckles of olive in her eyes told it all.

"Find out for yourself, nigga. I'm up." The ball I

needed was being used, so I opted for a smaller one and ended up striking. "You up!"

"Sosa. This is Brielle. Brielle, Sosa," Gauge introduced us to one another. I recalled the name being mentioned in her initial message, which meant she was the one that Gauge was trying to contact.

"Mr. Group Chat." Brielle smiled.

"Sosa. As she mentioned," I corrected, not a fan of pet names.

"Sosa." Brielle nodded. "Okay, Gauge. You got you a feisty one."

"I'm sensing you prefer someone a bit more chill," Cayman interrupted.

"I like all kinds." Brielle shrugged. "There's no discrimination on my end. As long as they're not looking for commitment. Just tried that shit."

"Sounds like I'm the man for you then. You here alone?"

"Not exactly. I was invited by cowork—"

"Go get ya shit. I'm here with a few of my people. We in lanes five and six." Cayman was direct, shooting his shot and making the basket. Brielle was onboard. The look in her eyes said it all.

"I wouldn't exactly call that laid back, but I'll take it. Mili, call me in the morning. I won't keep your date waiting. Love you, babes."

"Love you more." The two embraced before Gauge grabbed the ball of choice. "Are you always this mean?" she asked as Cayman walked off.

"I'm just me, G."

"You're pretty damn intense, Sosa. Brielle means no harm."

"I never said she did. I think you're in some feelings that aren't appropriate at the moment. As you wouldn't want your friend to change to accommodate me, I won't change to accommodate her. All is good. She seems like cool peeps from the messages I've gotten. But still. I can't be anyone but myself, regardless of who that rubs the wrong way."

"You're right. You just seem... so uptight when people—"

"Ain't a people person. Not even my homie got a warm welcome from me. That's just the way it is."

"Well, you seem quite accommodating to me."

"To you, G. I'm accommodating to anyone I want to fuck." Bluntness had always been my strong suit. Sugarcoating wasn't a task I had mastered, yet.

"Excuse me?" Her small, button nose curved, and the center of her forehead dented as her cheeks rose and mouth dropped.

"Don't be so surprised. It's a thing that women and men do," I reminded her with a chuckle, my easiness seeming to cause an issue as well. While she was uptight, my posture nor demeanor had been altered.

"And that is all that you want from me?" Gauge was disgusted with my confession, but it was truthful, and that's all she'd get from me. The truth.

"Na. If that was it, then we wouldn't have made it

41

off of the porch. I'm a resourceful man. I get what I want." Shaking my head, I encouraged her to take her turn.

"So what exactly do you want? Because I'm quite confused. I thought you only wanted to take me out on a date." She wouldn't let up.

"Yeah. Take you out on a date and then fuck." I shrugged.

"That'll never happen," she sassed, grabbing her purse and heading for the exit.

If that makes you feel any better, I'll let you think that. I followed behind her, happy that our time at the alley had come to a screeching halt. This date wasn't a social affair, and I wasn't up for unnecessary conversation.

"I can't even believe you'd think I'd stoop low enough to do such a thing. Fuck you on the first date? That's absurd."

GAUGE

"Ma, is you gone suck it or not?" His tenor was low and desperate. It was his second time asking, jarring me from my sudden slumber and reminding me that we had crossed that mark, and there was no recanting. He'd been relentless in his pursuit, but it wasn't as if I didn't want to oblige anyway.

I'd fussed the entire way home, refusing to let him

walk me to my door, but he'd made his way up the walkway anyhow. After confessing my displeasure for his rudeness and inconsideration, I found myself lip locked and insanely aroused as Sosa planted firm kisses on my neck while admitting that he had better usage for my mouth.

"I may actually like you," he'd sprung on me in the heat of the moment. "And once I give you something to calm your little ass down, I can apologize for my inconsideration—as you call it. And possibly make it up to you by letting you choose the venue on our second date tomorrow."

"I'm not going anywhere with you tomorrow."

"After you get this dick tonight, you will."

I'd wanted to put up a greater fight, but the way my body responded to him was foreign. His large hands caressed my pussy as he finalized our last activity for the night. I was kicking my own ass for waking up in the morning and regretting it, and I hadn't even gone through with the act yet.

Of course, I let him inside and strip me of my clothes before pressing my hands against the door and forcing me to bend my back. The jolly rancher he'd been sucking on felt like a little pill as he inserted it into my pussy with his tongue. As he sucked on my pussy from behind, he'd let it marinate.

The warmth of my walls melted it, and the sweetness came oozing from my tunnel as my orgasm overwhelmed me to the point of immobility. Not only could I not move, but my legs had given out on me. For a brief second, I passed out. When I woke, Sosa was standing over me with his dick tapping my top lip.

"Open up. Let me feed him to you." My lips were moist, allowing him to rub his thickness across them with ease.

He laid me across the couch after collapsing and propped a pillow underneath my head. I wasn't the one to administer head while laying down. Control was feasted on during my sexual encounters, and this one would be no different.

Grabbing the base of his dick with my right hand, I conjured a glob of spit from the back of my mouth and sent it flying onto his dark meat. As I gave him time to adjust to the introduction of my state-of-the-art blow job, I maneuvered until my knees were on the ground, and I was looking up at him.

The intensity in his eyes was humbling as he communicated that I'd be needing a lot more neck and forehead sweat before he was merely pleased with my efforts. He'd knocked me out cold—for the record—so I knew that I had to come with it.

Summoning the saliva from the back of my throat, I spread it all over his dick with my tongue before pushing it into my mouth. A pretty big boy, Sosa was challenging, to say the least, but I welcomed it. My main focus was relaxing my throat and expanding it to accommodate his size.

Back and forward, I weaved my neck without the

assistance of my hand. Each stroke I committed with my mouth allowed me to push Sosa a bit further down my throat than the first time. By the twelfth pump, I was able to slide him down my throat until I reached his ball sack. My gag reflex didn't exist when I was on my knees.

"Shit!" Sosa exclaimed.

At that moment, I knew that I had him where I wanted him. From there on, I performed every trick I'd ever taught myself. Sucking dick was an art to me, and I took the artistry seriously. By the time I was ready to bring him to his climax, Sosa pulled himself from my mouth and demanded that I bend over the bed.

A sly smile crossed my saliva covered lips. I was a mess, and I didn't give one fuck. The wrapper of a condom sounded, relieving me. I was so caught up in the moment that I'd forgotten to grab one from my drawer.

"Na. Get on the bed." He had a change of heart.

His thick arms were stretched out across my stomach as he began massaging my breasts.

"Put 'em in," I advised him.

Obliging, Sosa rubbed his slippery, condom-covered dick up and down my slit repeatedly. I was becoming frustrated with the teasing, so I reached beneath me and grabbed a hold of his dick so that I could put it in myself. Sosa knew exactly what he was doing, and I had no time to play his childish games. I was beyond horny and ready to feel him inside of me.

The thought was too much to bear any longer. I needed to feel him.

Whap!

He smacked my hand, causing me to retract and shake it from the pain I immediately felt. Simultaneously, Sosa burst through my seeping hole gently, nearly tearing me in two. He pushed himself into me slowly yet forcefully until he was buried inside of me completely.

It felt like the stars had aligned, and my soul had lifted from my body to hover over me and thank me for the goodness we were currently experiencing. He'd filled me to the brim and stretched me wider than the sea it felt like. I didn't know if I should scream from the pain or embrace the pleasure that came along with it.

"Ahhhh. Baby." I moaned as we both savored the moment.

"Fuck me back," he commanded, pushing into me and then pulling back. That shit was driving me insane as I watched his chocolate skin dazzle in the darkness.

I obeyed, giving him exactly what he craved.

Pushing myself into Sosa, I moaned with each movement to relieve myself. I never thought it was possible for pain to feel so damned good. Our bodies moved in sync as our souls tied one another.

"This shit too motherfucking good," Sosa said. "I'm 'bout to fucking bust." I could feel the tip of his dick enlarge, hitting my spot with each stroke. I tasted the blood in my mouth as the pain from me biting my lips resonated at the same time I began to mount. Squeezing my lids together, I yelled out obscenities as I reached my pinnacle place.

"Fuck!" Sosa was quick to follow. "Shit, girl," he fussed.

After he'd discarded the condom, Sosa returned to my side, and we both rested to regain our strength.

"Baby girl, who taught you how to suck dick?" Sosa asked out of nowhere.

"Huh?" I was confused by his line of questioning.

"If you can *huh*, then you can hear. Who taught you how to suck dick?"

"My ex."

"Shit, which one? I'm sure you have more than—" He was wrong. I'd only been in a relationship with one man in my life. Others hadn't quite made it past the first date.

"I only have one, Sosa."

For the first time, he was genuinely surprised. "Yeah. I might have to either body that nigga or send him a thank you package."

"What?"

"Nothing. Come lock up. I'm about to be out."

"Say what?"

"It late as fuck, and I need to get some shut eye."

"And you can't do that right here."

"I ain't never trusted a bitch—a woman enough to close my eyes and get comfortable at her crib. I won't

47

start tonight. That head was good, but it wasn't that damn good."

"That's cool then. Let me get dressed too because I'm coming with you. This is not that. That hit it and quit it shit is played out. If you leaving, then we both leaving."

SOSA

I watched in disbelief. Gauge was dead ass about leaving with me, but she'd be highly disappointed because I was leaving alone. This wasn't my first run in the park, and I had no plans of switching shit up. We'd enjoyed ourselves, but this was where the night ended.

"I'll be back to scoop you up around eight tomorrow night." I couldn't believe I was attempting to reason with anyone. That shit didn't even sound right coming from my mouth.

"All of that is good to hear, and I'll be ready. But tonight... Tonight." She pointed toward the floor. "You're not about to just walk out of here like I was some booty call."

"You said that. Not me."

"Since you can hear so well, then why haven't you heard a thing I've said in the last few minutes? Either you're staying with me, or I'm coming with you."

"You're not coming to my house." She was blowing

me, but I couldn't help but chuckle at the fact that I was considering laying my ass back down.

"Then good, because I didn't feel like putting on any clothes or driving back home in the morning. You need a T-shirt or something to get comfortable?"

"I'm not staying at your house either."

"Well, you'd better choose one and make up your mind quick, Sosa."

"G, I need you to chill. You acting like I ain't made plans to see you tomorrow."

"That's not the point. I just... I just did all of that stuff with you, and now you're trying to force me to sleep alone because you ain't feeling it."

"Na. Because bitches can't be trusted, and that's no disrespect to you."

Why the fuck am I trying to explain myself, and why am I still here? I questioned, noticing that I hadn't moved a muscle and was still at the edge of her bed.

"You know what? It's fine. Don't worry about tomorrow, and let's forget about tonight. See your way out, Sosa."

With that, she stomped into the bathroom connected to her bedroom and slammed the door. Baby girl wasn't afraid to speak her mind, and I liked that shit. Any other female wouldn't give a damn about what I did or where I went after parlaying in their pussy for hours. When it was time to bounce, I never got any feedback or back talk.

Yet Gauge was ready to throw hands with a nigga

just because she didn't want to regret her actions any sooner than the morning. My walking out would've shined light on the decisions she'd made during the night. The tingling in my chest assured me that I didn't want to be the cause of her agony tonight—or any other night, to be frank.

That's why I removed my glock from the night-stand beside her bed and shoved it under the pillow that I'd been lying on. When she emerged from the bathroom with red-rimmed eyes and a stuffy nose, I knew I was in trouble. My first reaction was to comfort her.

Comfort her.

Comfort her?

Closing my eyes, I rubbed through my deep waves to refrain from even looking her way. The sight before me was disheartening and required feelings that I simply didn't have to offer. Everything in me told me to put my shit on and run without ever looking back, but I was cemented.

The opposite side of the bed shifted due to her weight as she climbed in with her back toward me. Her theatrics might've been comical if I weren't beating myself across the head for tossing my feet onto the soft mattress and scooting down until my neck touched the pillow.

"I can't stand crybabies, G," I warned, reaching over to pull her in.

"Just leave."

"Shut up." I grazed her skin with my fingers. She scooted out of my reach, pissing me off and making me reconsider my decision.

"Just leave, Sosa," she repeated, knowing damn well she wouldn't be able to remove herself from her feelings if I decided to get up and walk out.

Women acted as if it were the end of the world when men walked out after sex as if his staying would change the situation or make it better. It didn't matter if you fucked a nigga on the first night or after the first month; if he wanted to rock with you, then he would.

If anything, niggas were proud to get the pussy on the first night to make sure that it was worth putting up with the bullshit that came with the woman it was attached to in the long run. Same for women. They shouldn't be so caught up on first-night relations, as it would help them decide if their partner's dick would be worth the heartache niggas were sure to bring.

"You did all of that whining about me leaving. You better scoot your ass back, G."

The lamp that had been slightly illuminating the room went out, signaling the fact that she'd flipped the switch. A few seconds later, I felt her backside against me.

"Don't expect me to take ya ass out tomorrow. This is our second date," I informed her.

"Good."

FOUR

SOSA

I'd always been a man of my word, but I guess we were both saying shit we didn't mean. While Gauge was asleep, I crept out of her house just as the sun rose. The clock had just struck eight as I was pulling up to her place. I wasn't able to get through to her the one time I got the chance to call, and neither had she responded to the text I'd sent reminding her of the time I'd be coming for her.

To get my mind right, I'd faced two blunts and was taking the edge off by sipping on some Hennessy. Either I was bored as shit, or I was really digging baby girl, because I had no intentions of returning after putting dick down her throat last night. But as I crept out of her crib, I knew I'd be returning for sure. One of the main reasons was that I knew damn well she was tripping about my disappearance.

Admittedly, I enjoyed her energy and wanted to hear her bellowing my name for the second night in a row. I'd even come prepared for the fight she was about to put up. I stepped out of the car and made my way up to her door. Once I reached the porch, I noticed her coming out of the house, not paying much attention to what was going on around her. I notated the fact that she needed to be reminded of being cautious of her surroundings, especially with her being a woman living alone.

"Where you headed, G?"

She whipped around and watched me climb the three stairs before twisting her key in the opposite direction and scurrying into her home. The wooden door slammed just as I reached it. She was quick on her toes. That shit tickled me to my core.

Before I could knock on the door that she'd just slammed in my face, my cell began to ring. Screening my calls, I noticed it was coming from her cell. I immediately picked up.

"Open the door."

"I told you that you should forget about last night and scratch whatever plans you'd made for tonight."

"And I told you that I was still coming and to be dressed by eight."

"No, you didn't, because I would've assured you that I wouldn't be going anywhere with you. I blocked your number."

"What are you? Fifteen? Sixteen or some shit? You blocked my number?"

"You wanted to fuck, right? Cool. You've done that. Now that you've gotten what you wanted, there's no point in sticking around to make me feel better about myself." She had a point. *Why was I sticking around?* "I'm good with my decision. We fucked. That's it. Now, go about your business so that I can continue my journey to finding love and a wholesome relationship."

Visions of her lips wrapped around another nigga's tool had me seeing red. "With who? Niggas like ole boy that stood ya ass up?"

"In fact, that is exactly who. There's nothing wrong with second chances, right? I mean, you are expecting one, which is why you're at my door, right now."

As she spoke, I tuned her out while watching the silver Audi pull to the curb. A second later, the horn was honking. Rage budded in my chest as I tuned back into the conversation.

"After fucking with me, you don't get to downgrade. Fuck boys are off the menu. This nigga doesn't even have the decency to come retrieve you from the house and knock on the door. Is it too much of an inconvenience to stretch his legs?"

"Sosa!" she yelled. "I haven't exactly fucked with you. We had sex. That's it. Why are you blowing this up into something bigger than it is? It was you that admitted to wanting that. Not me."

"Well, now, I'm admitting that I want more."

Feeling like the sucker I'd been for her since picking her up the previous night, I rolled with it and disconnected the call. The second I turned to head down the steps, Gauge came flying out of the door.

"You'd better not." She wasn't a fool and knew exactly what was on my mind. This nigga had to go.

"Either I'm going to do it, or you're going to tell him yourself." I pointed toward the car. Noticing the nigga was still inside of his vehicle assured me that he was a pussy.

"Sosa, I never confirmed a date tonight," she reminded me.

"Na, you got me fucked up. If I ain't taking you out, then you can stay yo' ass in the house."

"I made plans." Gauge was growing frustrated with me, as I was with her.

"And I just cancelled them motherfuckers."

"Why are you acting like we're together or something?"

The words flew from her mouth and punctured my skin as if they were daggers. Childish enough, I responded and helped her recall the dramatic tears that she cried while thinking I would hit it and quit it. Though it had been the initial plan, I had come back. Now that I was here, she was on some bullshit.

"I'm acting the same way you were acting when you didn't want me to leave last night... Like we're together or something," I mimicked.

"How dare you?" Her nose scrunched, along with

the skin on her face. She was ticked, but I didn't give a shit.

"Man, really. I'm tripping. Do ya thang." Coming to my senses rather quickly, I made my way to my whip.

"Wait, wait. Hold up." Gauge locked her door and came rushing behind me.

"Nah, I'm good. Enjoy yourself." Not giving her a chance to catch up to me, I continued.

With that, I slid into my car and peeled out of her driveway. Not only was my temper elevated because she had gone against the grain but also because I wasn't a fan of my behavior in the last twenty-four hours. Known to keep shit at a minimum, I was doing the most and needed to put distance between this spontaneous situation and me.

GAUGE

I didn't even go on the damn date with Tyler. My plans had backfired, and I was left alone for the second night in a row. Only this time, I wasn't looking forward to Sosa saving my ass, because he wasn't even taking the calls I'd been making to him for the last three hours.

Both of them had gone to voicemail after a couple of rings. I'd only known him for approximately twenty-four hours, and I felt as if we were a couple who were experiencing separation after years of being together. The thought of him being upset was appealing when agreeing to go on the date with Tyler, but I wasn't so sure anymore.

Since he'd pulled out of my driveway, my heart had been heavy, and my thoughts had been preoccupied with those of him. It was a Sunday night, which meant that Sauni was preparing her little ones for school the next morning. Brielle, there wasn't any telling where she might've been. Her breakup had given her the wings she never knew she had. I was genuinely happy for her. After being on lockdown for so many years, she deserved some freedom and fun.

Speaking of the devil, my cell buzzed with an incoming call from her just as I decided to shower and call it a night. "Hello?"

"Hey. What's up? How did everything go?"

Brielle was aware of my plan and had encouraged it. Sauni had warned me against it, but I wasn't willing to take the higher route this time. Sosa's entitlement was disgusting and had rubbed me the wrong way. I wasn't sure whom he'd been fraternizing with before me, but I was a different breed.

Other women may have been uncertain about their desires, but I knew exactly what I wanted. If he couldn't deliver, then it was best that he moved out of the way for someone who could. Our fucking wasn't the end all, be all. I'd gotten over it the minute I woke and realized he was gone. The three-way call with my girls this morning had also put a lot into perspective for me. I'd been dick deprived for over a year, so that beat down was well deserved.

"Horribly wrong. Now, I feel bad for the boy. He looked like he'd lost his best friend, leaving my house."

"He'll be alright. Call him."

"I have. For the last three hours. I have an eight o'clock in the morning, so I need to call it a night. Maybe he will come around. Maybe he won't. It was only one night."

"According to you, it was one unforgettable night. Even if you don't want anything with him, at least you need to be on the nigga's good side in case you need some dick."

"I'll be fine."

"Keep saying that shit until you be around here scratching like Pookie off *New Jack City*."

"Brielle."

"I'm just saying."

"Speaking of which, how was your date with ole boy?"

"Girl. Date? I'm not looking to date. I'm looking for a good time, and we both understand that. After bowling, we went to a little after-hour spot that I was calling to ask if you wanted to go to. They have the best cheese eggs and pancakes. It's only eleven. I promise to have you back before one. I'm starving."

"Are you only going to the spot because you think he'll be there? Sounds fishy to me."

"I know he'll be there. He's the one who invited me, but I'm not interested in going alone. It be mad niggas up there. Maybe you can snag another to replace that damn lunatic you're dealing with."

"He's no lunatic."

"He's not. He's thugged the fuck out, and I'm down with that," Brielle confirmed what I already knew.

"Of course, you are. Can you send me the location? Because I'm not riding with you. If your new boo is in attendance, then you won't be ready to leave when I am... which will be after I eat."

"Have your way. I'm leaving out of the house now. I'll text you the address. Thanks, friend."

"Bye, Brielle."

Instead of keeping on the clothes that I was currently wearing, I decided on a pair of navy tights and a white button down that stopped above my navel. I paired the simple fit with the Balenciaga sneakers that had come in the mail three days prior. With graduation in a few weeks, it was a gift to myself for sticking it out and finishing my Bachelor's degree with a 4.0 GPA.

Brielle had sent the address like she said she would, giving me the okay to leave as well. The little breakfast spot was only fourteen minutes from my house, so I was the first on the lot. As she'd mentioned, it was jumping, and it seemed to be more niggas inside than females. The large glass windows gave me a straight and narrow view inside of the diner.

"Gauge!" The peck on my window startled me from my thoughts. I'd absentmindedly began searching the parking lot for Sosa's car. A part of me had only agreed to neglect sleep, thinking that he'd possibly be with his friend.

"You scared me." I rolled the window down as I admired my friend's cute setup.

She was rocking some high-waist denim, a bejeweled fanny pack, a plum crop top, and some plum Nike Air Max. Her body was sickening, putting my little curves to shame. Needless to say, she flaunted them every chance she got, and I couldn't be mad at her.

"You look cute," I admitted. "Step back, boo. Let me get out."

"And you talking about I look cute. Where are these tights from? That ass looking like an entire entrée. Tits for dessert. Where's your bra?"

"At home where I left it." I shrugged.

We walked into the diner, which I'd learned to be Theo's Place, and took our seats in the far-left corner where we could see all of the action. Amongst the group of men that were posted to the far right, I noticed Sosa's friend.

"He's kind of handsome, Brielle. Maybe you two can work your way on past the friend status."

"I'll leave that to you and your lunatic." Brielle checked her appearance in the handheld mirror. "I'll be right back. Let me go see what this nigga is on."

I watched as she strutted over toward the table

before being pulled into Cayman's lap. Even though she didn't want to admit it, I knew that smile from anywhere. She liked him. With her pain still fresh, I was aware that she wouldn't jump into anything, but that didn't keep me from wishing her the best. Brielle was such a good person, and to know she was hurting was agonizing for me.

"May I help you?" I hadn't noticed the waitress's presence until I heard her voice.

"Yes. I'll take four scrambled eggs with cheese, lots of it, please. I'd also like a stack of pancakes. How many does it come with?"

"Three."

"Three sounds good."

"Anything else for you?"

"Can I have the same thing for my friend with two orange juices, please?"

"Coming right up. Can I take your menus, please?"

"Sure." I handed her the two menus that we'd never even touched.

Brielle returned with a smirk, causing me to question her motive. Either she was about to announce her departure or give me some detail on a conversation she'd just had that I probably wanted no parts of hearing. There was no telling with her.

"So."

"So what, Brielle?"

She paused to accept the orange juice that the

waitress had brought us both out. "So Cayman just got a call."

"And why does this concern me?" I slid the straw I'd unwrapped into the juice in front of me.

"According to what I heard, he just pulled up."

"And you're telling me this because?"

"Because you want to know, bitch. Don't act like you didn't come only because you thought he'd be here already. You don't do Sunday nights for anyone. *Anyone!*"

Before responding, I chuckled. I'd been caught red-handed. "So maybe you have a point there."

"Exactly. I was just giving you a heads up." Brielle slid back out of the booth. "I'll be back when the food comes."

"Just to be frank, if I feel the least bit discomforted, I'm leaving."

"Or if he mentions sliding down that dick again, you're leaving. I understand, girl."

"Go away." I waved her off. My friend knew me so well.

With the way Sosa was swinging that hood wood, I'd burn rubber getting back to my house if he wanted us to indulge in one another again. I couldn't deny my sexual attraction to him. It didn't help that he was savagely addictive.

"Umm. Hmmm. Don't front for me."

The minute Brielle stepped off, I began watching the door through my peripheral while knocking the edge off my nervousness by playing the word search game I'd downloaded on my phone to calm my anxiety. My nerve endings were shot, feet tapping against the floor and teeth chattering against one another.

For a split second, I figured I should put myself out of my misery and go home for bed, but just as I rose from my seat, the waitress appeared. As she placed our plates on the table, I noticed the red ensemble I'd seen hours prior stroll through the door. The lump of dry air that had clogged my throat nearly took my entire cup of orange juice to shrink before I was able to rid myself of it.

My eyes combed over his entire frame, flashbacks of the previous night causing a stirring in my under-wear. Surely, I'd made a mess of myself. I could feel the stickiness in the seat of them. I assumed he'd felt the effects of my gazing because the first direction his eyes followed was mine. We locked eyes for a brief second before he slid his tongue across his top teeth and lifted the right side of his top lip as if he were disgusted with my presence.

It was obvious he was pissed, but that didn't stop him from checking me out. I wanted to stand and twirl for his ass since he couldn't seem to take his eyes off me. I broke contact, assuring the waitress that we wouldn't be needing anything else for the time being. When my head rose, again from checking out my plate, Sosa had disappeared.

Instantly, my eyes roamed the entire diner in

search of him. When they finally landed, I wasn't pleased with their discovery. Up at the counter and sitting in one of the bar stools, Sosa and I locked eyes as he wrapped his arms around a young woman I guessed he'd met up with. His hands moved down toward her ass and didn't stop until he was under her cheeks.

The barf that rose up my throat was swallowed back, causing me to scrunch my face due to the bitterness and burn I tasted. I wouldn't make it through my meal. I wouldn't even make it through the next few minutes, so I grabbed my phone to text Brielle and let her know.

SOSA

From a distance, I could feel the anger radiating from her beautiful chestnut skin as she pecked away at the keys on her cell. To the far left was her girl, the thick bitch whose ass was grinding against my partner's lap. Like clockwork, she put her phone to her face the minute she received a notification. A second later, she was looking in my direction. I nodded and held my spiked orange juice up a bit.

"Where the hell you been?" Kimberly questioned.

She was an around-the-way girl who claimed to have kept her shit exclusive for me until she realized I wasn't looking for anything serious. Strangely, I'd relayed the message upfront. After busting her ass down in broad daylight in the back of her ride the first day I met her, I thought she knew what was up.

Any woman who lacked respect for herself couldn't get that shit from me. I'd have been a bit more understanding if she'd invited me to her crib, but she was too desperate and didn't want to fuck up the opportunity to get with me. It was shit like that that made me question everything women stood for and keep them at a distance. But the woman that was currently tossing money on the table to pay for an untouched meal had me questioning my own damn self.

Focusing on the table full of niggas and a few bitches they were fucking, I contemplated going after her. The thought vanished as I reasoned with myself. Forever cautious, I refused to show any signs of interest in anything or anyone for a few reasons. For starters, attachment was a sign of weakness in the game.

The minute you exposed your weakness, you became open season for the cops and the robbers. Even if niggas weren't plotting now, they'd know where to start whenever they did. The last thing I wanted was to give motherfuckers ammunition to take shots.

So I remained seated as she stood from her booth and stormed out. I watched through the window to make sure she got to her car safely. Watching her speed out of the parking lot had been comical, especially since she'd just come from a date with some ole lame ass nigga.

"That's you?" Kimberly reminded me that she was present.

"That's none of your fucking business. You trying to put them lips to better use?"

"If you've got a job for them, they're willing to take it."

"Call me in about an hour. Let me holler at my people. Step off."

With a smile on her face, she obliged and joined her friends at the other end of the counter where she was when I'd walked inside. Cayman rose as he witnessed Kimberly step away. Nodding, I encouraged him to bring his little sidekick with him. I had a few questions for her about her bipolar ass friend. Cayman's face covered in perplexity, but he demanded that she join us anyway.

"Let me holler at her really quick, Caym," I announced once they'd made their way over.

"Aight. I'm going to take a piss."

Once we were alone, I began. "What is her problem?"

"I don't know, exactly."

"You're her friend, and you don't know." Scratching the side of my face, I stared back at her with questioning eyes.

She'd rested her cell phone on the counter, giving me the right to it. I picked it up, which caused her to move forward and get the first fair warning.

"Don't." I put a single finger in the air.

"Why do you have my phone?"

"Because I saw her text you before she left. Since you can't tell me what her issue is, then I'll find out myself."

"I highly doubt it. My phone is locked. So if you don't mind, hand it back."

"I mind," I informed her following the fingerprints on her screen to enter her code. So predictable. Flipping the screen around, I showed her the text thread she was currently engaged in with Gauge.

"I see you've got some sense. Why doesn't your friend listen to you?"

In the few messages that I read before exiting the messaging application, I saw that Brielle was encouraging Gauge to approach me instead of leaving. Apparently, she wanted Gauge to confess to the fact that she had plotted the date in revenge and ended up cancelling it once I showed my face. As well, she'd warned of her the side effects of losing good dick. From the looks of it, Brielle was suffering from a loss herself.

Checking her recent calls, I was partially stunned by the amount of times Cayman had reached out to her. There wasn't a single outgoing call to his cell. That nigga was hooked. I could smell that shit on him when he walked his ass over. Putting thoughts of their fling to the side, I dialed Gauge's number, knowing that my shit was blocked.

She answered on the second ring. "I can't stand that fine ass nigga. I swear."

"Good, because I can't stand you either. Where you at? I'm coming to you."

"Fuck you, Sosa."

"I can arrange that," I fed into her theatrics. "Where are you?"

"On your goddamn mind."

"I'll catch up with you."

She didn't give me a chance to say anything else before disconnecting the call. Gauge was a bold motherfucker, if I must say so myself. Not only was she reckless at the mouth, but she had no boundaries, and fear was absent of her body. That shit made my dick stand. I had yet to meet anyone—woman or man—on Earth who felt comfortable enough to speak to me in such a hostile manner.

"She mentioned an eight o'clock tomorrow."

"She's in college. It's her last year."

"What school does she attend?"

"SMU."

We went back and forth as I garnered information that I hadn't known previously. Gauge wasn't just as intriguing as she looked. According to Brielle, she'd be graduating in the upcoming weeks and had been a student at SMU for the last four years. It all made sense. Her crib was only about eight minutes away from the campus. Knowing that exams and shit were coming up as well as her early class the following morning, I cancelled my plans of pursuing her. She was a good girl, and I wouldn't bring shit but chaos to her little world. I wasn't ashamed to admit that I was fucked up like that. The only thing that followed me was trouble.

"Appreciate you."

Brielle wasn't as thrilled returning to her seat as she had been on her way over.

FIVE

GAUGE

As I strutted through campus grounds on my way to have a cup of coffee before my next exam, I noticed the deep-red Bentley that I'd seen on the picture Sosa had sent to our group message a while ago. It couldn't be mistaken, not with the custom wheels and man in red sitting on the roof with smoke floating from his lips and into the air. Sosa was unbelievable.

Two weeks. That's how much time had elapsed before I heard anything else from Sosa. Certainly, his presence was delightful, but the last thing I needed at the moment was to be distracted. Instead of continuing my path, I cut through the grass and decided against the coffee after all. Seeing him would put enough on my mind to keep me awake during the hour-long exam I had at twelve.

As the thick shards of grass ate away at my

ankles, I could hear footsteps behind me. They were closing in as I tried picking up my pace. I'd completely forgotten the length of his legs and the fact that two of my steps amounted to one of his. Within seconds, I was being flung around and slung into a solid chest.

Damn, I missed this nigga, I confessed, but not a peep left my lips. With his arm around my neck and face buried in my hair, he inhaled. I felt him tighten around me as I tried maneuvering from within his grasp.

"Did you miss a nigga?" he questioned, reading my thoughts.

"Let me go," I demanded.

"I tried," he spoke of an act more complex than the physical of which I was speaking of. "I tried."

"Then try harder."

"Let me talk to you." Finally letting up, Sosa held me at arm's length.

"About what, Sosa? There's nothing for us to talk about. Let's be honest here. I don't even know you. You—"

"Sosa Giyani Law," he spoke, cutting my off.

"What?"

"Twenty-seven-year-old, dope-slanging, gun-toting nigga straight from Oak Cliff. I ain't the most social nigga, but I've been wanting to socialize with you. Never had a bitch. No kids. No crazy stalkers. Pops doing a bid. Moms died when I was nineteen. Low-key.

Introverted at best. I prefer my lonesomeness, but you've been making a nigga reconsider."

"Why are you telling me all of this?"

"Because I don't need any more excuses for you to avoid me. Now that you know me, can I get to know you?"

"Seeing as though you know where I go to school, where I live, and my schedule... I'd say that you know me well enough."

"Good, then. On to the next phase."

"Sosa."

"What? May as well speed this shit up." He shrugged, letting me go. "Now, you gon' let me walk you to your next class, or you want to grab a bite to eat, first."

"You smell like weed, Sosa."

"And half of these professors 'bout smell like dope. I used to make my rounds up here. Know the campus like the back of my hand."

"Mr. Law, please."

"I'm just keeping it one-hunnid, Gauge Miliani Morrison."

"Wow. Inspector gadget."

"Nah, nothing close. Food?" he questioned.

"Coffee and a bagel, possibly." Nodding, I began walking toward the student center.

"Whatever you want, under one condition."

"What's that?"

"Unblock my fucking number or end up phoneless."

"Are you really this damn crazy in real life?"

"I'm not. You just need to change your way of thinking." I felt his arm as he flung it across my shoulder.

As promised, Sosa waited with me until my next exam started. Before departing, we made plans to see one another again. Surprisingly, I'd been invited to his home to watch the second round of the NBA playoffs with him since I didn't have the channel, and he would rather not go to the bar.

I'D DRESSED THE PART, pairing an old school Jersey with a pair of biker shorts and tennis shoes. When I arrived at Sosa's home, I was in utter disbelief. It was nothing short of amazing. The modern adobe was equipped with a state-of-the-art security system that put me through hell while simply trying to get through the gates. I wasn't surprised to see the fleet of red cars aligned behind a floor-to-ceiling glass enclosure. At the center of the spiral drive was the red Honda I'd seen all too much of.

Sosa opened the door of his home as I exited my own car, a pearl Lexus with tinted windows. His smile was intoxicating, even without the grill in his mouth. There was something about a man who cared for his teeth that drove me up the wall, or maybe it was only Sosa. Either way, I was enchanted.

"Did you have trouble locating my spot?"

"Given that the gate is a million feet tall, I thought that you'd led me to the wrong place."

The gate that surrounded Sosa's home was huge. From behind it, you couldn't see his massive home or any of the land surrounding it. It would be impossible for anyone to get over it if they ever attempted.

"Na. I saw you driving around in circles and started to call."

"You saw me?"

"I see everything, G. Come inside."

Sosa extended his arm to usher me inside of his home. I'd expected to see a common red theme but was surprised to find the subtle browns, grays, and blues throughout his home as we continued toward the large opening furnished with couches and a wall-to-wall television.

The screen was enormous, topping any that I had ever seen. "Geez. What size television is this?"

"Hell if I know. It's custom. Do you want anything to drink? Eat?"

"I'll have something to drink. Make it fruity, and don't put nothing in my cup that'll have me waking up and wondering where I am."

"Why would I need to spike your drink when I already done had the pussy? Tasted it? Know what it feels like? Know how it sounds when it's wet? Know how it feels when it's gripping and 'bout to—"

"Sosa. Do you really have to get so deep?"

"I do." His mind was in the gutter.

"You know what... Just go ahead and fix that drink."

"I'll be right back. Get out of them shoes and make yourself comfortable."

SOSA

Bullets were what I was sweating. I'd never entertained a woman in my home—or anyone, for the matter. The only feet that had graced my marble floors were mine and those of my construction crew. As I gathered the two drinks to return to the sports room, I prayed Gauge had taken her ass to sleep. I didn't give a damn if she'd just gotten here. To my dismay, she was bright-eyed when I reentered.

"What's in here?" she questioned, grabbing her cup and taking a sip.

"You done already hit it now. What does it matter?"

"It doesn't. So fill me in. Who are we rooting for, and what's going on so far?"

Women. "I'm going for Golden State. Had you come on time, then you wouldn't have missed the entire game. We in the third quarter now."

"You specifically said to come when I felt like it as long as it was after seven because that's when the game came on."

"And you chose damn near nine?"

"Well, you live a million miles out, Sosa." She had a point, so I let up on her. "And why are you sweating?"

"Me?"

"I'm not talking about me. Come sit down. Rest those long legs of yours."

Finals were over, and Gauge had admitted to the exhaustion she felt due to the stress of them and her pending graduation. While life for me was hectic as shit at the moment, I decided to invite her to invade my privacy.

Instead of taking a seat on the couch beside her, I chose the ottoman. My comfort was extremely altered with another pulse residing in my home for the night. I hadn't neglected to see the overnight bag she'd brought with her.

Gauge made her own rules—because I knew damn well I hadn't mentioned spending the night. The thought alone had me reconsidering the invitation I'd given. Neither of us knew the results of baby steps, because we were both jumping right into whatever the hell we were doing.

"What's the matter with you?" Scooting toward the edge of the couch and spreading her legs so that I was between them, Gauge placed her hands on my shoulders. "Why are you so uptight all of a sudden?" She began kneading away the kinks that were present, forcing me to relax a bit. "Talk to me."

Her motive was obvious. Gauge wanted to get into this head of mine, but I'd be damned. The weight of the world was on my shoulders, but I'd be damned if I let her in. Two niggas from the crew had gotten popped on some silly shit, and I was left to worry if they had turned state. My attempts to get on the inside had failed, no one accepting the hefty note that I was willing to pay in order to receive information from the inside.

For months, I'd been trying to convince someone on the force that being an ally would be insanely beneficial to them, but most felt threatened by their involvement with me and claimed that it would possibly put their families at risk. Bullshit. I didn't fuck with families. If I had an issue, I got rid of the source. Picking off family members, frightening wives and children, it wasn't my thing. A problem of yours wasn't a problem of theirs.

"Who told you that you were spending the night?"

"Me," she stated boldly. "And I'd appreciate it if you didn't fight me on this, because I'm going to win. You saw what happened last time."

"I felt sorry for your crybaby ass. That's it."

"It won't take much for me to cry again."

"Oh, so that was all an act?" I chuckled.

She paused. "No. Actually, it wasn't. I think I may

have been so stressed with school and then getting stood up. You trying to vacate kind of was the tip of the iceberg. I don't know why, but it hurt my feelings."

"I'm so—" I caught myself.

Yeah. She'd have to go in the morning and never return. I nearly found myself apologizing for someone else's mistake. Frankly, I hadn't done a damn thing wrong. I took her out and gave her the good dick I knew she needed. My deed was done. "I'm so happy these niggas ain't letting up. If they don't watch it, Harden gon' push through on their asses," I redirected my statement.

As I felt her continue pressuring my shoulders, I relaxed a bit more. In an uncomfortable silence, we both watched the remainder of the game with her massaging my shoulders, arms, and hands. The shit felt so good that I was only minutes away from sleep.

"So, we won?" Gauge asked as the buzzer sounded.

"We won." I nodded.

"Good." Taking her drink to the head, she emptied the cup and returned it to the table that it had been sitting on. "I think I'm going to get out of here now."

I sensed the sadness in her tone and the sluggishness her posture. She didn't want to leave, and the thought of her walking out of the door somehow irritated me. Just thirty minutes prior, she was campaigning to stay. I didn't quite understand where the sudden change had stemmed from.

"Gauge, if you don't sit ya lil' ass down some

fucking where." I pulled her back down to the couch she'd stood from.

"I think it is best that I leave, Sosa." She stared back at me.

"Why?" I didn't want to care why she'd flipped in a matter of minutes, but I did. Recalling our conversation, I tried thinking of what I'd said to steer her in this direction.

"Because. This all seems... awkward. I mean, you wouldn't even join me on the couch after I invited you to. Besides the conversation that I've initiated, you haven't said one word to me. You haven't even touched me since I've been here."

"You sound really fucking spoiled right now, G. The game was on. What was I supposed to be doing? Help me out here. This shit new to me."

"I don't know. You just seem so distant."

"Because I am."

"Then why invite me over, Sosa?"

"Shit, I don't know. I ain't seen you in two weeks, and that little hour that I got with you this morning wasn't enough. I knew the game was coming on tonight, and it was the only down time I had, so I decided to involve you. Fuck, why the hell am I explaining myself? Been doing this shit for the last few weeks."

"Because you should. It's called communication, and it is what two people need for understanding. Why is my presence such a huge deal?"

"There's a few answers to that question. We'd need more time."

"I can wait." She folded her arms across her chest. Now, leaving didn't sound so daunting after all.

"Besides the motherfuckers that built this house, no one has ever stepped foot inside. I don't trust anyone. Not a fucking soul."

"But you trust me."

"I'on even trust myself sometime, G."

She scoffed. "And what is that supposed to mean?"

"I don't have to spell it out for you. Let's not make this an issue. You're here, so that's saying a lot."

"What is it saying? That you want to fuck again?"

"I could've done that shit at yo' crib. I ain't that pressed over pussy to jeopardize my safety. Ya shit good, but it ain't that damn good. Let's keep this shit a hunnid."

"Then it doesn't say much else, Sosa."

"Possibly that I like ya stubborn ass, and I've never been able to say that shit about nobody. No woman walking God's green earth can admit to that shit. I'm offering something to you that I perceive as my most valuable aspect of life. Something motherfuckers can merely get minutes of. *My time.*"

"Stop trying to find something to fuss about and just chill. I ain't them lame ass niggas you prefer, nor do I know anything about this dating shit, but give a nigga some kind of credit. I'm trying. And if you were to compare my lifelong commitment to not fucking with too tough or getting attached to women, then you'd understand that I'm doing a hell of a job defying that mentality."

"But what I'm not going to do is kiss ya ass. Either you fucking with me or not. I'm just not trying to deprive myself of the first thing that has felt good to me besides getting money. That's it. So maybe you should take the night to figure your shit out, because I'm in no rush to fool around with uncertainty."

"I'm not uncertain. I know what I want."

"Then what is it?"

She had been saying this since the beginning, but I was beginning to doubt it.

"You." I could hardly hear her response, so I made her say it again. Uncertainty. That was the only thing that would explain her lowered head and voice.

"What? 'Cause I can't hear you with ya head hanging."

"You, Sosa." She stared me in the face, not blinking or folding.

"Then that's that. You got me." I shrugged. There was no more to it.

"Sosa, it doesn't work like that. It's not that simple."

"Why can't it be? It's as simple as we make it. You want me, so I'm yours."

"But what abou—"

"You want me, so I'm yours."

"Until you decide that you're bored with me?" She wanted to make something out of nothing, and I didn't understand why. No, I was no relationship expert, but I knew that it didn't have to be as complicated as moth-erfuckers made it.

"Until my casket drops." Maybe she didn't believe me, but I'd always been better with demonstration.

"I don't think you understand," G tried to convince me, but I wasn't hearing her shit.

"I just figured it out. What's so hard about the deci-sion to keep someone in your life?"

"Sosa, you said you've never done this before, so you have no idea—"

"And you have but still didn't get it right. I say that we try a new way because the by-the-book shit ain't guaranteed either."

"You're killing me here." Her frustration was obvi-ous, but I didn't give a fuck.

"I want you in my life, G, so that is where you'll be."

"But at what capacity, though?"

"Whatever capacity you want, G."

"Maybe I want something you can't give me."

"If I got it to give, you can have it."

"Trust." She hit below the belt.

I chuckled.

"And love."

I shook my head.

"And marriage," she continued. "And four babies."

I could see where this was going, so I decided to end her theatrics. "We can worry about the other shit at a later date. Let's start with the basics. How many babies you said?" Leaning forward, I took her bottom lip into my mouth as I began rotating my fingers against the fabric of her shorts. "Four? Let's see if we can kill two birds with one stone."

"Sosa."

"Shut up, G." I lifted from the ottoman and forced her back onto the couch. "Take that shit off. I want to see you play with it."

GAUGE

"Shit, baby." I arched my back and rubbed my pussy faster.

"That's it, baby girl," Sosa encouraged.

I was near my mark. He waited beside me with his dick in his hand as he stroked it nice and slowly. The thought of having him inside of me drove me insane. I'd tried several times to reach out and grab him but was unsuccessful. Since he wanted to be a tease, I was going to put his dick inside of me myself. I tried focusing, but his movements were so distracting.

"Imagine me sticking this dick all up in you," he coached, taking me back down memory lane to when we first fucked. I could feel him entering me all over again.

"Baby." I rubbed even faster. "I'm going to cum."

I closed my eyes as the orgasmic wave hit me like a

ton of bricks. Simultaneously, I felt Sosa enter me, giving me every inch of his big, black dick. Arching my back, I nearly rose from the couch.

"Fuck!" he chastised. "I ain't got no fucking condom."

He'd picked a fine time to mention it. Now that he was inside of me, there was no turning back. The damage had been done. I sensed he noted the same when he began hitting me with those death strokes of his that left me breathless.

Once he got himself going, I pushed forward, and so did Sosa. Our bodies became one as we searched for each other's souls once again to tie the knot. I threw my head back as Sosa slid in and out of me. The juices from inside of my tunnel coated his black dick. Each time he pulled out, it got a bit creamier. Pretty soon, his dick was unrecognizable, and it sounded as if he'd been stirring a pot of saucy macaroni.

My wetness assisted him in his mission to go even deeper. His plunges lengthened, and his strokes intensified. Literally, Sosa was swimming in my pussy.

"Yes... Yes... Right there," I moaned, encouraging him not to let up off of my spot.

He felt so good inside of me. I knew that I would be back for more each chance I got. This was the type of dick that sent a woman to the nut house if it ever stopped coming around. I was in no rush to the insane asylum.

Sosa brought his hand up toward my neck and

slightly grabbed it, wrapping his hand completely around it. Steadying himself, he leaned forward and bit my neck. "I need you to cum again!" Sosa was on a mission and wouldn't stop until he completed it. I wouldn't deny him of his satisfaction, so I maneuvered so that my pussy received the perfect amount of friction.

"Yes..." With labored breathing, I bellowed, "Don't stop!"

"I won't. Remember that shit." He looked deep into my eyes as he stated his claim. "You hear me?"

"Yes! Fuck! Fuck!" I repeated as Sosa tore into me over and over again.

"Cum for daddy," he coached, bringing me back to reality.

"I-I'm cumming."

Simultaneously, we gave into instant gratification. Underneath Sosa, I melted. Dick this good should've been deemed illegal a long time ago. Even with a sore pussy and exhausted frame, I wanted more of him. I wanted as much as I could consume and then to over-dose on the rest. I'd never get enough. Not ever.

After our steamy session on the couch, we enjoyed another round in the shower and then in his king-size bed. I was in love with Sosa's home. Though large, it was lonely. Without a doubt, I knew that it was where I wanted to spend most of my time.

"All of this space and no one to share it with."

"Who said that?"

"The walls. I hear them talking," I clowned as we shared the bed. Contentment was apparent as I lay in his arms.

"Na. Ask them motherfuckers the same questions around this time next month. I bet they have a different answer."

"Ummm. Hmmmm."

"I've never been in the business of convincing. Either you believe this shit, or you don't. Your choice."

"I believe you, Sosa." And I did.

"Good, now take your ass to sleep. You done wore a nigga out."

"Goodnight." I chuckled as I felt him pull me closer. In his arms, I felt at peace.

SIX

GAUGE

"G, I need to make a run." Darkness was everywhere as I stirred from my slumber to a fully dressed Sosa. Since the night I'd come to his home three weeks ago, I hadn't left.

"Why?"

"Because I've got some shit I need to handle. You gon' be good?" Concern was etched in his tone. Even in his toughness and rugged edges, Sosa was so attentive to my needs or even the thought of them.

"I'm tired."

"I know. Go back to sleep."

We'd stayed awake all night, exploring one another's bodies as if we hadn't been for the last month. Sosa had the type of dick that strung you out and stressed you out if he ever decided to remove that shit from your life. I'd met the man only five weeks prior and knew that I'd die a slow death if he ever denied me of his dick. His persona was even more addictive, holding me captive as if he were practicing mind control over me.

But what felt the best was the reciprocation. I wasn't the only addict in the house. Sosa demanded my presence and desired me just as much as I did him. He was slowly getting through the awkwardness of companionship, but he was doing well. My only concern was his willingness to speed into our situation rather than walk slowly. However, our thing still felt damn good.

"Sosa," I called out as I felt him vanishing. Near the bedroom door, he called out to me.

"What's up? You need anything before I leave."

"No."

"Then what's up?"

"Come back to me," I declared. Honestly, I didn't want him to leave. He never left in the middle of the night, always at my side when I decided to scoot over or toss my limbs over him.

I rolled over, expecting to hear his footsteps creeping out of the door, but they came closer. Sosa hurried to the bedside and flipped me back over onto my back.

"What did you say?"

"I said come back to me."

"Fuck it. I'm not going anywhere." I heard him wrestling with his clothes before climbing back into bed.

"What are you doing? I thought you had a run to make?"

"This may sound crazy." He rotated my body until I was facing him. Through the darkness, I could only see the white of his eyes and teeth.

"I'm sure it won't. What is it, baby?" I was exhausted, but Sosa's sudden disinterest in handling his business had me concerned.

"For the last few months, I've been having the same dream. It always ends with me getting smoked. Before I left the house, my wife—who I have in the dream—has parting words for me. Guess what they are?"

"I love you?" My brows furrowed.

"Come back to me." He sighed. "That shit you just said."

"Get out of here."

"For real. And guess what her name was?"

"What?"

"Millie."

"Mili? As in what my friends call me? As in my middle name?"

"Yes. And I've been leery about this little meeting all fucking day. I feel like your words were forewarning me of some shit that could pop off."

"Sosa, you're scaring me."

"Nothing to be scared of, G. You always trying to get up in this head of mine, so I'm letting you in. Go back to sleep. I'm going to be right here." Sosa pulled me into his chest and planted his hand in my hair. He was aware that head rubs, as well as booty rubs, put me right to bed.

SOSA

"Gauge. I've got shit to do. Call one of your home-girls and have them come through for you."

"No. I was very specific in my request, Sosa. I want you to come with me." I watched in defeat as Gauge pranced around the bedroom in a pair of panties. As she pulled her shirt over her head, I lost track of my thoughts.

"Whoever go with you, I know you're not wearing that shit."

She'd been bringing clothes over each time she came to my house for the night. I'd cleared a section of my closet and was sharing my dresser with her now. Shit was changing for me, and I couldn't say that I regretted allowing her into my space... into my life. It was taking some getting used to, but it felt natural. Like she belonged here all along.

"Reach in that top drawer and get a damn bra."

"You don't wear bras with shirts like this."

"Then choose another shirt."

"Why? You afraid someone going to get a big idea and come for what's yours?" She thought everything was a joke.

"Na, I don't want you moping around the house 'cause you were the cause of a nigga getting his top let back."

"Well, we will just have to see."

"G, stop playing. I'm dead ass. Get a bra or change shirts." She ignored me and began pulling up the gray tights she had laid out on the bed. "And you think you wearing them shits with ya ass and stomach out? You 'bout to get somebody bodied. I swear."

Gauge had picked up a few pounds, thanks to the good grown man dick I was breaking her ass off with every night, morning, and any other chance I got. I could tell she was feeling herself because her clothes were a bit more revealing, or maybe it was because the changing of the weather. I didn't know, and neither did I care. Something would have to give, or somebody was getting killed.

"You know what..." Standing from the bed, I tossed my shirt over my head and headed to the closet to retrieve a pair of jeans. Business would have to wait. I'd rather skip a meet up than plan a homicide behind G.

"Put on your shoes. We're not staying in the galleria all day. I don't even shop at the fucking mall." The thought of being around so many motherfuckers was maddening, but I wasn't sending Gauge out alone.

"Now you're not going to start rushing me because you're upset."

"Gauge, if you know what's best for you, you'd chill."

"Or what? You gon' cry?"

"Na, I'm going to give you something else to do with that big mouth of yours."

"Just say the word, Papi, and I'm down. Literally. On my knees. Mouth open. Throat waiting. Spit conjuring. Pussy dripping. All that."

She was such a freak. As smart as she was, she was the nastiest woman I'd ever encountered. Sometimes, I considered knocking her ass up just to claim that pussy for at least the next eighteen years. Gauge was the type of woman you expected to have mediocre skills, possibly a bit above average. Yet, she amazed me each time we were intimate. There had been several times she'd made me tap out, lulling my ass to sleep like a newborn.

"You could barely walk this morning. I suggest you chill and bring your ass on."

"So feisty. I'll buy you something. I promise."

"With my money? Oh. Big shit."

Gauge had awakened to a purse filled to the brim with stacks, yet she still wasn't satisfied. Giving her the money wasn't enough. It was my time that she required, opting to pay for her own graduation fit if it meant me going shopping with her. In the end, she'd be getting money and my time, two things I'd vowed to never give a bitch.

"It is the thought that counts. I could always spend it all on myself."

"Trust me. You ain't spending all that in one trip to the mall."

"Try me." She smiled. "There is Gucci inside The Galleria, Sosa."

"Believe me. You not spending all of that shit in one setting."

"How much did you really give me?" She faced me, now concerned.

"Enough to get you through the next year of shopping with your habits."

Gauge didn't require much. She was simple. The only expensive piece she had was a pair of Balenciaga sneaks. Besides that, her wardrobe was lightweight.

"Stop playing."

"I'm serious. You ready or what?"

"How much is in that purse, Sosa?"

"Each stack is a thousand dollars, Gauge. I'll let you figure that out."

"There's tons of them in there. That's a big purse. I know you didn't."

"I did. Now, let's go."

"Maybe I should leave some here, put some up for safety measures."

"If a nigga even steps close to you, I'm blowing his ass off. Don't put nothing up. You good."

GAUGE

There were fifty stacks in my purse. Fifty. Ten hundred-dollar bills in each, wrapped in a rubber band, and connected to larger stacks that equaled ten thousand dollars each. Even with all of the money in my purse—that Sosa considered as my graduation gift—he still came out of his pocket to purchase my things each time we went to the cash register. Of course, I'd only spent a measly three hundred dollars before we were both ready to go. I'd found the perfect dress and Steve Madden pumps to match. I stopped by Victoria's Secret and got a little thank you gift for Sosa, courtesy of his pockets as well.

"See. That wasn't so bad, huh?"

"It wasn't, but I'm starving, G. Let's see what's up with this sub shop."

Sosa led me into the brightly lit sub shop. As we stood in line, we both began surveying the menu to see what we'd be eating. The blaring of a cell phone caught my attention for a second, but I refocused once realizing it wasn't mine or Sosa's.

However, I was startled by the baritone greeting the caller on the other end of the phone. I knew that voice from anywhere. The hairs on the back of my neck stood straight in the air as I recalled the many days it had rung loudly in my ear. Justin. I'd been with him enough years to identify his voice out of a crowd.

While the first few years of our relationship were peachy, the final two were hell. It began with verbal abuse that stemmed to mental and then physical. The final straw was when Justin pushed me down the stairs of my dormitory while a freshman in college. After that, it was a wrap for us. He was the main reason I decided not to live on campus anymore. Seeing him every day was agonizing, especially watching him descend after our breakup. Within a year, he'd quit the football team and had dropped out.

"G." Sosa had been calling my name, and though I'd heard him all three times, I couldn't respond. My mind had traveled to a faraway place. Bizarrely, the fear that I experienced as a teenager came to the forefront.

"Gauge." He raised his voice, causing Justin to twirl in search of me. He didn't have to look for long, because I was right behind him.

With a menacing smile, he nodded his head. "What's up, Gauge?"

"Shit." Sosa didn't give me a chance to respond, as if I could, anyway.

Justin's eyes followed the length of Sosa's frame until he reached his eyes. I shuffled my weight from one side of my body to the other, praying that both men behaved themselves. Justin obviously didn't want the confusion Sosa was ready to bring to him, because he stood down.

"Pay attention, nigga. You up next." For so many reasons, I felt as if there was an underlying meaning to Sosa's heads up.

When Justin moved up in line, Sosa grabbed my

arm gently and led me toward the back of the restaurant. "Who is he?"

"What are you talking about?"

"Who is he, G? I'm not feeling the way you tensing up around this nigga. I'm ready to rock his ass to sleep. Tell me. Who is he?" Sosa didn't miss a thing. The damn man paid too much attention to detail.

"He's my ex-boyfriend, Sos." I referred to him by the pet name I'd given him.

"Him being an ex ain't a good enough excuse for you to be so uptight around him. You nearly jumped out of your skin when you heard his voice. What did he do to you?"

"Sos..."

"You want me to trust you..." Leaning down, he gritted in my ear. "Tell me what this nigga got you scared for." I lifted my head, and he stared into my eyes and waited for a response. "If you are going to lie, I swear you can find a way back home, and I'll have your things brought to you. I have a zero tolerance for liars, G."

"I wasn't about to lie," I admitted. "He... uh. He was abusive. I broke up with him because he pushed me down a set of stairs, and I broke my hip."

First there was pain.

Then there was sadness.

Next was disbelief.

Afterward was anger.

The final look in Sosa's eyes was unbearable. The

stoned expression caused me to worry about his mental stability. I reached for him, but he snatched back, causing me to catch the button of his shirt.

"Please. Let's just go."

"Na, G. Gone head to the car. Here's the valet ticket."

"Sosa."

"Don't say my name, G."

"Listen. It was so long ago. I'm fine now. Everything is good."

"You scared of that pussy ass nigga. Ain't shit good on my end. When you're with me, there ain't a motherfucker on God's green earth that should be able to pump fear in you. If I'm not willing to be the one, then no one else will stand in the way of your peace either. Here. Take your bags and go get the car."

"I'm not leaving, so—" I halted. "I'm not leaving."

"Then you can watch me drop this nigga then."

Soundlessly, Sosa pulled his pants up on his waist before stepping back over toward the counter. Justin had ordered his food and was waiting in line for it to be prepared. He had no idea that he was in some deep shit, and I was silently praying that Sosa took it easy on him. Not for his sake but for mine.

"Say, my nigga," Sosa started. "Let me holler at you right quick." He was fuming but attempted to remain calm.

"I'm getting my food. Whatever you want, I'm sure it can wait."

Before speaking again, Sosa chuckled. "Na, partner, this is an urgent matter. Either you walking out this bitch with me, or I'm dragging you out this bitch. Either is cool with me."

"Say what?" Justin questioned with a smug look on his face. His eyes darted over to where I stood with questioning eyes.

"I'm the one to focus on, player. Don't even look in her direction. I'm really doing too much talking. Either you coming, or I'm bringing you myself."

"I ain't going—"

Wham.

Sosa rammed Justin's head into the glass that protected the customer's food as the workers prepared it. It reminded me of the glass caging that secured the food at subway. I cringed, swallowing the huge lump in my throat at the sound of it.

Justin slid to the ground like a limp ragdoll. The store manager ran from behind the counter in an uproar. Leaving Justin on the floor, Sosa tended to the manager, who was in his personal space.

"Ain't shit to drop you too. I suggest you stand down, amigo."

The Spanish gibberish he began chanting was the least of Sosa's concerns as he began to drag Justin out by his shirt.

Quickly, I followed behind them to see where Sosa was headed. When we reached the escalator, I understood where this was going. I prayed to the heavens that I'd been smart enough to remove Sosa's gun from his waist when I realized he planned to confront Justin for his wrongdoings. The first move he made was for his piece.

Noticing it wasn't where he'd left it, Sosa's head whipped around until our eyes locked. An eternity elapsed as we connected on a million more levels than we had before. Silently, we communicated what we'd both been attempting to disown—the love we shared for one another.

Lifting his size twelve feet, Sosa pushed forward and sent Justin flying down the escalator, causing anyone in his path to lose their balance and tumble with him. Without a word, Sosa grabbed the bags from my hand and started for the exit.

Thankfully, valet hadn't parked the car in the garage. It was posted outside by the large fountain for spectators to admire. We got inside and sped into traffic. The agonizing silence was causing frustration in the worst way. The minute I realized we were headed to my home instead of his was when I decided to speak up.

"Why are we going to my house?"

Sosa remained quiet, not even preferring music to fill the empty space. There was no need in asking him the same question, because I knew he wouldn't answer. At this point, it was best to let him be. When he was ready, he'd give me the answer I needed.

Ten minutes after the initial question, we were

pulling up at my place. I was the first to exit the car with Sosa hot on my trail. It didn't matter how upset he was with me; he was always the perfect gentleman. He toted the bags inside after I'd unlocked the door.

"Give me my piece," he fussed.

"I will once you tell me why you're upset with me."

"I don't have time to play these childish ass games, G. Give me my shit so that I can roll."

"Sos, you need to chill. I haven't done anything for you to be so upset with me."

Within seconds, he'd rushed to my side. He'd been all the way across the living room, on his way out of the door. I watched his nostrils flare as my pussy thudded, waiting for his next move. There wasn't an ounce of fear in me, knowing that Sosa would never do anything to harm me physically. He'd lose his mind if he did.

"You wanted this shit." There was a disturbance in his voice.

"What are you talking about, Sosa?" I didn't understand what he meant.

"You got exactly what the fuck you wanted. I fell right into your little sick ass trap. Played your game and gave your little spoiled ass your way."

"You're going to have to be more specific. I don't—"

"You wanted me to fall in love with your stubborn ass, didn't it?"

His tone was menacing with hues of disgust tagging along through his delivery. This wasn't what he wanted. It was written all over his face. My heart threatened to beat its way out of my chest as I stood in silence, not sure how to respond.

While I'd expected to be basking in the afterglow of his confession one day—under less stressful circumstances—I was wishing that I'd never entered the wrong number that day. But even the thought of never encountering him pained worse than knowing his preference wasn't to love me.

"I just nearly bodied a man in broad daylight in a fucking mall with spectators because you bitched up around him. That's the exact reason I stay away from this shit. I could've brought so much unnecessary attention my way for this dumb ass shit."

Sosa shoved my body forward until my back was against the wall. He ripped the gray tights I'd worn out to shreds before doing the same to my satin underwear. My arms wrapped around his neck instinctively while still under great distress from his previous confession. I felt his enlarged manhood enter my most sacred space, the one that he'd claimed due to his selfishness.

Up and down, he stroked me as if he were going for broke. Deep, long, calculated strokes that broke my heart a bit more with each one. Soundlessly, Sosa was relaying a message to me, fucking me as if he'd never see me again because he probably wouldn't.

This wasn't makeup sex. This was the type of lovemaking soldiers delivered their wives before they went off to serve. This was the kind of pipe criminals laid down on their girl before going to do a bid. This was the type of sex that sealed fates and made goodbyes easier to fathom because one was still floating before the realization was apparent.

I rained on him, drenching him with my forgiveness, and he hadn't even come back yet. But I knew he would. If what he'd confessed was truthful, then there was no amount of risk that would deter his efforts. He'd come back to me. We were just getting started. He had no other choice. I felt his climax reaching as his strokes quickened, and his grip tightened.

"I can't do this shit, G," he confessed. "This shit gon' get a nigga fucked off. I'm sorry. I can't do this shit," Sosa whispered in my ear as he released himself into my awaiting oasis.

"You can," I encouraged him as my body went limp. The wetness that stained my face was evidence of my dissatisfaction with Sosa's revelation. "I know you can."

His strokes had discontinued as he leaned forward and buried his face in my hair. His labored breathing was music to my ears, pulling emotions from deep within that I'd harbored since the first time he'd cut off communication over a month ago.

"No, I can't. Any sign of weakness, and there's a target on my back. A target on yours." He began letting me down.

"I love you, Sosa." The tears were in abundance.

"Don't say that shit," he fussed, lowering my feet to

the floor. "I'll have ya shit brought to your house before long. I need some time to sort this shit out."

"Why are you so upset?" I had to know. "Why is it so frustrating to admit how you feel? What's the harm in admitting what—"

"Because, G. Niggas like me don't get to fall in love."

With a crumbled face, displaying his true feelings, Sosa reached forward and wiped the tears from my eyes. "That's just the way it is."

SEVEN

GAUGE

The bright morning sun shone through my window with cruel intentions. My eyes prickled, reminding me of the long night I'd spent alone. After a late rehearsal, I stopped by the liquor store and grabbed two bottles of Stella Rosa Black. Netflix had been my savior, allowing me to watch an unlimited stream of movies.

The Vow happened to be one, which left me crying, horny, and wishing Sosa would come around. It had been three days, and no word from him. The first two days, I'd blown his line down but decided to give it a rest last night. Now, I was sitting on the edge of my bed with a lousy hangover, wondering if he would come to my graduation as he'd promised weeks ago.

I continued replaying our last encounter over in my head to understand how I had become the issue suddenly. The misery that covered Sosa's face as he confessed his love for me was something I'd never forget. That shit haunted me in my sleep.

In all of my years, I'd never met a man so damned determined not to love. I understood that he was in the streets, but that was no excuse to run from the very thing that had been the reason for his existence—I was sure. Thoughts of him were becoming agonizing, so I tried pushing them to the back of the brain.

Today was about progression, starting with walking my ass across the stage after five-years of undergrad. I could've graduated last semester and stayed at the four-year mark, but I was two credits shy, which pushed my date back a full semester. Being that I was in no rush, I took my loss like a champ and continued pushing. I was on a full ride, academically outperforming my entire school body and graduating valedictorian of my high school. Again, I was in no rush to kick the books to the curb. After completing my undergrad, I had every intention of completing my Master's.

My alarm sounded as assurance that I was up and at it. With the way that my night had gone, I wasn't sure if I had the strength to wake myself without a bit of assistance. I shut it down before opening the messages I'd been receiving throughout the morning.

They were mostly from family, while others were from my two best friends. My father's message was the most heartening. He'd raised me alone, taking on the responsibility at only seventeen years old. My mother, whom I despised with great joy, had opted for adoption after begging my father for abortion money that he would not give her.

At the hospital, she insisted they give me up for adoption, being that she had her entire life ahead of her. She was only sixteen at the time. After discussing it with my grandparents, my father took sole custody of me, even omitting my mother's name from my birth certificate upon her request. When my father turned eighteen, and I began walking, my father was forced out of his parents' home and into the real world. It was tough love, and he thanked them for it every day.

When I turned fourteen, I met my mother for the first time. We happened to run into her at the grocery store while shopping for my birthday party. My father introduced her as my mother, and the look on her face spoke volumes. She hadn't expected him to, and neither had I. By now, I'd come up with my own theory. I'd repeated to my classmates and friends so many times that my mother died giving birth to me that I began to believe it myself. She was as good as dead to me. I didn't see her again until my high school graduation, where she made it clear that she wanted to establish a relationship with me, but I declined.

Every so often, she'd try slithering her way into my life, but I would shut it down the minute I got word. She'd been getting my father to do her dirty work, serving as the middleman and message deliverer. He'd always wanted us to make amends, but I didn't give a damn about that shit.

Quickly, I responded to every message I'd received with intentions to see everyone later. My father had reserved a section at Red Lobster for our large party, knowing that it was my favorite seafood spot. There would be fifteen of us, fourteen being that Sosa was MIA. Trying not to get too caught up in my feelings again, I headed for the shower.

***

SOSA

I watched my baby walk across the stage. As much as I wanted to disappear and not confirm my presence, I felt that I needed to let Gauge know that I'd kept my promise and showed. There were hundreds of graduates to be called after her, but I had moves to make. Finally, I'd gotten a detective on board and would be meeting him in an hour outside of Dallas.

Come here.

I texted, knowing she had her phone in her hand. Nearly the entire student body did. I waited as the gray bubble appeared before she responded. Taking a peek at my surroundings, I tried figuring out where the hell I was, knowing that she'd ask.

G: You're here? Where?

Instead of explaining, I took a few pictures before sending them out. Gauge responded with the quickness. She let me know that she'd come but couldn't stay long.

G: *I'm coming, but I only have about five or ten minutes to spare.*

I may not even have that long. I responded before sliding my phone inside of my pocket.

"Hey." She was so angelic, the complete opposite of the man before her.

Her soft nature reminded me of why she didn't belong in my world, a world filled with strife beyond one's wildest dreams. It was enough looking over my own shoulder. I didn't want to have to look over hers too. Besides, the feelings that I had for G were so immense that I would never subject her to the lifestyle I'd grown to love. It was all I knew.

I'd been in the streets since the age of sixteen and hadn't looked back. Tired of seeing my mother struggle, an empty dinner table, and no new shoes by the time the new school year started, I picked up my first piece of crack after taking the alleyway home and finding a dealer slain.

She was so beautiful, her hair straightened and the sparkly dress we'd agreed on hugging her curves. She had unfastened her robe to let some air inside. I was certain she was burning up in that thick motherfucker.

"What's good? You out of there."

Temptation led me to reach out to her and pull her into my chest. I hadn't shared an embrace with her since leaving her home a few days ago, and I was feeling the effects of it all. Each night I laid in the bed that she once occupied, I realized how special she actually was to me. The darkness that she'd lit had returned, and my lonesomeness was more apparent than ever.

Gauge had provided me with something intangible, something undeniable, something unforgettable. Her absence was devastation and far more notable than her presence. I was plain sick without her, but I'd never admit it. Not to her, and especially not to anyone else. So I held my shit together while showcasing the genuine happiness I had for her.

"Yeah." I tried removing myself from her space, but she wasn't ready. "G." I pried us apart. "You good?"

The waterworks began. I hadn't intended to make her cry. "Maybe I shouldn't have called you out here. I just wanted to let you know I'd kept my promise. Let me get out of your hair."

"No. I'll be fine. It's just that... this is all so new to me. Have you had enough time to sort things out?"

"G, not today."

"I really need to know, Sos. I'm sick about this." She wiped her tears. "I miss you."

"I miss you too," I admitted, assisting her in wiping her tears.

They were swords through my chest. "Are you coming to dinner too?"

"Na, G. I just wanted to see you walk and give you these." I reached into my back pocket and retrieved the envelop.

"What's that?"

"Dry your eyes, and I'll let you open it," I bribed, desperate for her to dry those tears that were spilling from her beautiful eyes.

"Okay." Gauge straightened her face and posture.

"Here."

She tore the flap and pulled out the contents. Inside were three tickets to New York with the plane leaving in the morning. We'd made plans to drive to Houston that no longer existed, so I was certain she'd be free.

"Sosa." She began jumping up and down. "You didn't."

"I did. Go enjoy your girls. There's a debit card in there as well that I loaded with money. Everything is on me. Make sure that I got their information correct. If not, then I can give you my travel agent's information to get the shit straightened out. I've got to run, G. I'll see you around." Pulling her by the chin, I kissed her forehead and then her cheek. "I'm proud of you, baby girl."

With that, I disappeared into the small crowd of people walking about. Once I made it to the door, I could still feel her presence. Turning around, I noticed she hadn't moved from the spot she'd been standing in. Giving into my flesh, I circled back around.

"I'm sorry," were the only words that came to mind as I pulled her into my arms and savored her essence. "Go back inside, G."

On the hour journey outside of the city, I contemplated busting a U-turn and being at Gauge's side. But that shit wasn't happening. The travel station that I had agreed to meet the detective that would be on my team was equipped with a Subway in which we'd be conducting business. Once I was parked at the far end of the lot, I pulled the hoodie over my head and slid the dark shades onto my face.

"Detective Lancer," I greeted, sitting at the table next to the one he was perched at. With our backs toward one another, he began.

"Evening, Mr. Law. I have a few files for you to look over. The lead detective on your case is squeaky clean. I've tried to get dirt on her, but I'm coming up empty-handed. Her partner, however, Mansfield, has a bit of a coke habit. He's adamant about keeping his shit under the rug. He doesn't score. He ruffs up the local dope boys and takes what they have on them. Seen it with my own eyes."

"How much do they have on me? Did Fonzo and Whim sing or what?"

"They don't have enough to convict you of anything right now. It's all just a theory. They're scrambling to find information, but no one talked."

I would spare their lives. "Appreciate it. Put the files in the second stall of the men's room. I'll be in right behind you."

GAUGE

"Look what I got, bitches!" I whispered to my friends as we all settled in our seats at the long table.

My father, Sauni, her twin girls, her husband, Brielle, my grandmother Lorraine, a friend I met in school named Audrey, and a host of others had gathered after my graduation to celebrate my accomplishment.

"Where are you going?" Brielle asked.

"Where are *we* going is the question. Sos got us tickets to New York. We head out tomorrow. Sauni, do you think that you'll be able to get away?"

"As much as I need this damn girl's trip, my husband had better comply, or I'm divorcing his ass."

"We both know that is a lie, but we will let you have that." Brielle shrugged.

"Seriously, I'm in. How long?"

"A week, but we can rearrange your flight if you need to be back early. I know it's such short notice."

"No, ma'am. Count me in. Between my mother, mother-in-law, and grandparents, the girls will be just fine. Hell, they can alternate days for all I care. I'm tired."

My girl was raising two beautiful babies and caring for her husband without complaint. She deserved some time away, and I was thrilled that she'd be able to get that. I couldn't wait to get to New York and show the hell out. Sosa might not have been talking to me at the moment, but I planned to spend his money like he was.

"Mili. Come here, baby," I heard my father call out to me.

I stood and skipped over to where he was seated near my grandparents. My father didn't look a day over thirty, and it was hard to believe that he was my dad. When anyone saw us out together, they assumed we were a couple until we told them otherwise.

He was such a loving and kind spirit. I couldn't remember a time when he'd even yelled at me. Many predicted he'd fail as a single father, while people like my grandparents were rooting him on from the sidelines. I was so happy to prove to everyone who'd counted him out that he'd raised a good one. Giving him something to brag about was my life's mission.

"What's up, old man?" I pulled out the extra seat next to him.

"Nothing, I just wanted to tell you how proud I am of you again. You know how many times I quit college and how many student loans I racked up. I didn't give two snips, though. I used that refund to provide us with a roof over our head and food in our mouths. Looking back, I'd say that it was all worth it."

My grandparents nodded and agreed. "Every other year, you were enrolling somewhere." My grandmother chuckled.

Their genes were dominant. I resembled my grandmother in her younger days so much that it was uncanny. However, I didn't mind seeing how I'd age beforehand. She was simply the more mature version of myself, and she aged like fine wine.

"Really?"

"Yeah. One time, he even found a community college that had a daycare. While he skipped class to work, you were taken care of."

"See. It all worked itself out." My father grinned. "Whatever it took, I was willing to do."

"And look what came of it all." My grandmother patted me on the knee before grabbing my hand.

I could feel the cash she had clutched in her palm, warming me up inside. She was the sweetest, and I loved gifts from her. They were the most thoughtful and most forgotten at the same time. She always gave me jumbo packs of socks that I always loved. Another gift of hers was pajamas, which I wore the threads loose on. There was a plethora of others that I wouldn't think to gift anyone, but they surely came in handy.

Thank you, I mouthed.

"I need to use the ladies' room. I will be back. Don't order without me, guys!" I yelled to the remainder of my guests.

My bladder felt as if it were about to burst at any minute. I stood from my seat and followed the restroom sign until I was pushing the door open and rushing into a stall. Luckily, the restroom was very clean and consumer friendly. I pulled a seat cover from the box and placed it beneath me as I sat.

"Ahhhh." The sensation that rushed through me as

I released a stream of urine was inexplicable. After I was done, I handled my hygiene and exited the restroom. On the way out, I bumped into a budded chest, which caused me to stumble backward a bit.

"My apology—" I started.

"Gauge?" The unfamiliar tone caused me to inquire about its messenger.

"Do I know you?" I questioned.

"Yes." Removing the shades from her face, I recognized the woman in question as my womb donor. She'd given me life and decided against being in mine. "I'm your mother."

"Na, you shouldn't use that word so loosely. Try womb donor. I wouldn't even call myself a mom if I was you."

"How long will you punish me for my past mistakes."

"As long as that shit hurts! And, frankly, I highly doubt if that'll ever not be the case. Excuse me. I have people waiting on me."

"I know," she admitted.

"Did your sick ass follow us here?"

"I wanted to congratulate you."

"For what? You didn't play a single damn role in this degree. Exactly what is the point of you congratulating me for? The only congratulations that matters is that of my loved ones, the people who have been on this journey with me."

"I've been here, Gauge. Just in the shadows."

"Then why make your presence known now?"

"My intentions weren't to upset you."

"Then you shouldn't have come." I shrugged. "I suggest you leave."

"I just want to talk."

"Talk about what? Man, if you don't get the fuck out of my face, I'm going to have an entire episode."

"Gauge, please. I didn't come to cause a scene"— because that's exactly what we were causing—"I hope to hear from you one day. I'll be waiting. Your father has my number."

"He's been had it, and I ain't used the shit yet!" I yelled to her as she fled.

My whole damn mood had changed. The nerve of her! I was livid as I made my way back to the table where my father was. From the look on my face, he could sense my discomfort.

"I need to speak with you," I mumbled in his ear.

Immediately, he was up on his feet and following me to a more secluded area. "Everything okay?"

"Is she on a mission to ruin my life?" The anger formed tears. "Why won't she just leave me alone?"

"Mili." He softened, pulling me into his arms and hugging me as he had in the past. "Listen, she knows she fucked up, Mili. She regrets the shit. I get messages from her every so often begging me to get you to try and talk with her. I keep reminding her that these things take time. If you never decide to talk to her in your life, I stand with you. If you decided to call her on tomorrow, I'd happily give you her number. She's not a horrible person, Mili. Understand that."

"When she tried coming into your life after she'd matured, I kept her away for the both of our sanity. You didn't deserve the pain that her presence would cause. You were too young, and I wanted you to be able to make that decision for yourself. Now that you're older, the power is in your hands. Use it how you see fit, love. I'm with you either way. But I do suggest you talk to her so that you can let go of this pain you're feeling. I don't like it one bit."

"Me either. I'm just not ready."

"Then don't give it any thought. When the time comes, you'll know. For now, let us just enjoy this dinner. It's your day, and I refuse to let her get you down. Don't ever let anyone rob you of your joy. It's not theirs to have."

"You're right."

"Come on. Your people are starving after that long ass graduation ceremony. I'm about to get full off of biscuits if I don't order soon."

I followed my father back to the table where we celebrated without anymore hiccups. I was so happy to be surrounded by the people I loved, but the gaping hole in my chest wouldn't allow me to forget that Sosa was missing.

I COULD HARDLY SLEEP last night. I'd gotten home around eleven after Brielle and I stopped by a bar and loaded up on drinks. Sauni would've joined us, but she had to begin arrangements for our departure. By the time I made it home, I was toasted but still needed to pack a few things and clean my home. By the time I laid down for bed, it was two in the morning.

As we boarded the flight, I was paying for the long night and three shots I'd had. Brielle was all smiles, walking through the airport as if the sun shone on her ass. As big as it was, it probably did. First class was a breath of fresh air. We were able to board almost immediately and didn't have to concern ourselves with the rush that came with boarding flights. By the time everyone else piled onto the plane, we were seated and buckled in.

There were only two seats to a row, and we all had our own. Sosa had somehow gotten the seats next to each of us as well. I wasn't sure how he'd worked that out, but the flight attendant assured me that the seat was reserved for my comfort. I didn't argue, and neither did my girls. Exhausted, we all stretched out and slept through nearly the entire flight.

One by one, we woke a mere hour before landing in New York. "Sauni, you awake?"

"Yeah. I haven't had this much peace since I had the girls. Lord knows it takes weeks for me to finish a good book. If I could just relax by somebody's pool and finish this latest *Gray* novel, then my trip would be made. I've been sleeping on this author, but I'm woke now."

"I don't want to see another book for at least the next six months." I chuckled.

I, too, had a fetish for good books, but school got in the way of my hobby. Now, I was lucky to complete three in a year. It was pathetic, but it was life.

"I feel you. Brielle loud ass sleep. Good. She'd wake the entire plane up." I observed, taking a peek back at her row.

"Baby, don't worry about me. Worry about getting the flight attendant's attention so that I can get some more damn liquor." Her eyes were closed, but that heffa was definitely awake.

"Try some water, Ms. Thirsty," I suggested.

"Hungry but never thirsty, boo. There is a difference."

"And you don't know it, obviously," Sauni joked.

"Fuck both of y'all, really."

Another forty minutes of shit talking, and we were landing. Again, we were the firsts off the plane and headed to some unknown destination. Both Sauni and I were surprised to see a sign with my name displayed across it when we reached the baggage claim area to retrieve our bags.

"I'on know what you surprised for. That's the shit that you get when fucking with a boss." Brielle chuckled, handing her bag to the man who was encouraging us to put them down so that he could take them.

"And this what I get for fucking with a bug-a-boo." She sighed. "This nigga heard I was going to be gone for a week and nearly flipped a wig like I'm his bitch. Nigga, I'm free as a fucking bird. Stop trying to lock down some shit that can't be tamed. Especially not after the shit I just went through," Brielle fussed as she pecked away at her phone. "Five text messages. Who does this shit?"

"You like him, Brielle," Sauni pointed out.

"No, I like his money and the good dick he is slanging. He's merely entertainment. I'm not trying to catch a million bodies just because I'm single. I just want him to understand that this shit is just fun for me. I'm not in no rush to be nothing more than what we are—fuck buddies."

"Well, you never know. Maybe it can blossom into something beautiful," I encouraged.

"Same shit I thought last time."

"You have a point there." I agreed. "Do you know where we are going?" I addressed our driver as we walked out to the car.

"Yes. Downtown Manhattan," he confirmed.

"Sounds like a plan to me."

We piled in the back of the car, all well rested and ready to see what New York had to offer us. When we arrived at the hotel, I was partially at a loss for words. Sosa had gone out of his way to bring me the joy that his presence had stolen, and it was working.

"Reservation for Gauge Morrison," I spoke to the receptionist.

"Ms. Morrison, I have your keys right here and ready to go. You can leave your bags here, and someone will bring them up for you. Would you ladies like a glass of champagne?"

"I'll have two." Brielle was the first to speak.

We all indulged in the bitter champagne that we could live without while being ushered to our room. While on the elevator, I paid close attention to the number of floors we were passing. Once we reached the thirtieth, the hairs on the back of my neck began to rise. There were only ten more floors left. Of course, we passed them all up and landed on the top floor, which housed two penthouses, one on either side of the hallway.

"Ms. Morrison." The bellman held the elevator open, and we all stepped out. "This is you."

I inserted the key into the door to gain access of the room. When I opened it, my mouth slacked, and my eyes bulged from their sockets. I'd been in a handful of hotels throughout my adult life, but none of them compared to the three-bedroom penthouse that I'd be occupying for the next week. Forgetting that my friends were behind me, I let the door close, but Sauni was able to catch it before it smacked her in the face.

The bellman was the last to come inside. "Should I give you guys a tour?"

"Yes," I replied with glee.

We covered each room of the penthouse, following along and listening intently. The first room to cover was the common area. It was open and spacious, equipped with a full kitchen and bar. Next were the bedrooms, which all had bathrooms attached. There were floor-to-ceiling windows, but neither opened. The bellman explained the suicide rate in New York city and how their hotel was taking necessary precautions to prevent it. I respected it, but it would've been nice to step out onto a balcony and enjoy the city's skyline.

Once we were all settled in, we met back in the living room to pop the bottle of Ace that was waiting on ice when we got in. I couldn't help but keep checking my cell. I'd sent Sosa a message thanking him for his generosity. I was completely overwhelmed, and this was only day one. With our flutes filled and in the air, we toasted to our girl's trip.

"To New York!" I screamed.

"To New York!" my girls followed.

EIGHT

SOSA

The screeching sound of my alarm stirred me from my slumber. I'd been studying case files for the better half of the night. My restlessness had me on edge, mainly due to the fact that I wasn't alone in my home. The sound of clinking, nailing, hammering, sawing, digging, and yelling should've been enough to keep me awake.

My construction crew was on duty throughout the night and had been for six months now. The only time they were able to rest was the first night I'd invited Gauge over, who happened to be the one who'd triggered my alarm system. In a pair of basketball shorts and a tank, I opened the door. Thanks to my reflexes, I caught Gauge before she went crashing onto the ground.

"I'm baaack," she slurred.

"Gauge. It's only been two days. You were supposed to be gone a week." My nostrils flared, anger budding in my chest because I knew that she could've been seriously injured or worse in an accident while trying to get her drunk ass to my house. "Why the fuck didn't you just call me? Who let you drive like this?"

"I came back because I had something to tell you." She ignored my question, pissing me off even more. Them bird ass friends she had weren't supposed to let her get this sloppy, and neither were they supposed to let her drive. I had something to tell them hoes when I caught up to them. Gauge was in no condition to stand, let alone drive.

"H... Hey. I love you. Hey. Look at me." Sober thoughts.

Gauge was cutting away at my anger with her words and sultry look. "I'm taking you to bed."

"Boss, is everything alright?" Julio appeared in the foyer.

He was in charge of the construction to my home. At his side was a M249, a pretty ass automatic that would knock the head off of a lion if need be. Though large and extremely lengthy, the machine gun was light in weight but fulfilled its duty just as the heavier pieces I owned.

"Julio."

Gauge was familiar with Julio only because she'd been a great host during her time here and continued to stuff the workers with her meals to the point that the itis would kick in, and progress would slow. I'd directly forbade contact between her and the workers, but Gauge was Gauge. That shit flew out of the window once she realized they would be around often.

"Hola," Julio greeted her, his face absent of a smile and waiting for a command.

"Stand down, Julio. It's only Gauge. I wasn't expecting her."

"I'll get back to work."

"Julio, tell this man that I love him."

I'd never seen her so off her square. The fact that she hadn't been in my presence for protection during her alcohol consumption period had me furious. "Gauge, shut the fuck up. I'm taking you to bed!"

"Please take me to bed, daddy. Punish this pussy because I've been a bad, bad girl tonight. I almost gave it away."

Before I could catch myself, I'd removed my arm from around her. She plummeted to the ground in a fit of laughter. "He was a lousy kisser, so I knew he'd be a lousy fuck."

Her honesty was gruesome, gutting me like a fish and leaving my heart hanging outside of my chest. "So I had to come to where I know I can get some hood wood. I knew my Sos would take good care of me."

Kneeling beside her, I grabbed her chin and made her face me. I needed her to witness the venom she was injecting me with simply from her words. It felt as if my eyes were about to pop out of their sockets, veins bulging and trigger finger itching to pull something.

"Gauge, I will break your fucking face if I ever hear anything else about you and some other nigga."

"No, you won't." She chuckled.

She was right. The fact that she found my threats comical made me want to punish her ass. I scooped her into my arms and headed for the stairs. I took them two by two until I reached the bathroom.

"Are you going to give me a good spanking, daddy?" Gauge asked as we entered the master bathroom.

I lifted her onto the sink and started the water. No, I wouldn't put my hands on her, not ever. But that didn't mean I wasn't going to wash her fucking mouth out. She had broken every code of conduct I'd created for her, and the shit had me pissed. Na, I couldn't have her, but that didn't give any other nigga reason to think they could. This shit was mine. From her head to her toes, Gauge belonged to me, and I sure as hell belonged to her. A bitch couldn't touch my dick if her name wasn't Gauge Miliani Morrison. That was on everything. I wasn't even giving them conversation at this point. She had my head gone, which was why I had a bar of soap in my hand, swiping it across her lips while she tried slapping the scalp off of my head.

"Na, you want to dirty this motherfucker up, kissing niggas and shit."

"Stop!" Gauge fussed, getting down from the counter.

She increased the water pressure and began scooping it onto her face. I felt as if I were about to blow once I noticed the little dress she had on that was barely covering her ass. Too afraid to let my thoughts wander and risk talking myself into murking something, I decided to take my stress out on her pussy—my pussy. The only walls of confinement I'd ever agree to.

"Soooooooooos," Gauge moaned as I slid into her.

I pushed those panties to the side, too eager to get inside of her to consider pulling them down. She was home. I found more comfort in her than I did in the sheets that I slept in every night. She was my refuge, and I sought coverage each chance I got.

As I administered the first stroke, I confirmed the fact that I'd been out of my fucking mind, trying to tame the sprouting of my feelings for this damsel. This was life for me now, no matter how much it went against my beliefs. Gauge's presence wasn't to be undervalued or unappreciated, as it had been in the past two months. If I wanted to keep my head attached to my neck without losing it of complete mental breakage due to her finding a nigga worthy of her precious time, then I knew that the games ended tonight.

"Don't you ever..." Her box was wet for me, always had been. "Let another motherfucker put their hands or lips on what's mine. You hear me?"

"Yes, baby, I hear you." I watched as our bodies connected. The floor-length mirror to the side of us and the large one in front of us displayed our figures from several angles. Pulling her upward, I twisted her face until our lips touched. I didn't give a fuck about the traces of soap that lingered. Her flavor was more potent than anything I'd ever tasted.

"My fucking lips, aight?" I gritted, biting her bottom lip.

"Yes." She hissed in pain. "Yes."

"My pussy." Reaching forward, I cupped her pussy with my hand.

"Yes, it's yours." She nodded.

"My bitch." I stroked faster... harder.

"Okay."

"Say it." My hand snaked around her neck, pressuring it until she turned beet red. Gauge was as kinky as they came.

"I'm your bitch, Sos!" she screamed. "Bite me."

This wasn't for pleasure, and she couldn't have it her way. Her demands were null, and I surely wouldn't be granting them. Gauge needed to understand that she wasn't running shit, and that started with the lack of concern for her freaky ass fetishes. She hated when I ignored her wishes, so I did exactly that and continued pounding her pussy until I felt lightheaded, and my little men swam through her tunnel.

Fuck pulling out. I was ready for child support, spousal support, baby mama drama, and breast milk stains on the sheets if that meant keeping Gauge grounded and keeping her pussy on lock. I was able and willing to retire my sanity for the next eighteen years to keep baby girl around.

I'D JUST GOTTEN comfortable when I realized I hadn't received the message I'd been waiting for since falling accidentally asleep. With the construction crew gone and Gauge resting peacefully at my side, I could think clearly. My burner hadn't buzzed since Cayman confirmed that he was about to make his final drop of the night.

Throwing comfort to the wind, I jumped up from my bed and retrieved the small black flip phone that we used to contact one another. I had five of them laying around, each serving a different purpose, each programmed for a certain caller, each necessary.

Double checking the ringer to make sure that it was on, and I wouldn't miss any future messages, I tapped the volume button on the side. As I figured, the ringer was set to the highest volume. Concern consumed me. Immediately, I dialed Cayman's burner and waited for him to come through the line.

"Yo, we good?" I questioned the second he picked up.

There was silence on the other end with my question going unanswered. Perplexed, I removed the phone from my ear to make sure Cayman had answered. He had. Without further thought, I slammed the top of the phone down and tossed it onto the floor. Barefooted, I smashed it until the pieces were no longer recognizable. Something simply wasn't right with that call and Cayman's absence, and I felt that shit in my core.

Seated across from the bed, I stared through the dark as Gauge slept peacefully. Her hair was flawless, covering the pillows with a few strands flowing down her back, essentially a goddess calming the storm that was brewing within me.

My cell rang on the nightstand next to my side of the bed, jarring me from less complex thoughts of her. Slowly, I stalked over and retrieved it. The caller was unknown, but it had never stopped me from answering, so I proceeded.

"Yeah."

Seconds elapsed before the operator began speaking. "You have a call from..." There was a brief pause before his voice came over the speaker. "Cayman."

The line went dead after hearing all that I needed to hear. I immediately shut the phone down and started for my office. "Fuck."

My adrenaline was pumping, mind wandering, and feet moving a mile a minute it seemed. The lights glowed, welcoming me into my private office. On the desk was a small hammer I used more often than I'd like to. Each time I picked it up, a phone had to be replaced. The iPhone was no match as I hammered it before scooting the crumbs into the trash.

I snatched my top drawer open and removed one of the twelve iPhone boxes that were left. Every ninety days, I rotated cells. I still had a few weeks of life on the one I'd just crumbled, but I'd be damned if I got myself in a jam by trying to hold on to it.

As I powered up a new phone, my thoughts kept leading me back to the call I'd received. I couldn't understand why the hell Cayman would take the risk of calling the line that was absolutely legit. Worry was heavy, but the insurance we both had for one another kept me at bay. At lightning speed, I made a call to my lawyer and put him on. I needed Cayman to be released immediately, and didn't give a damn what he had to do to make that shit happen.

"Sos," I heard Gauge's voice.

The distress in her voice was apparent. Within seconds, I was at her side. "G, you good?"

"I need to puke." She began pushing the cover from her body.

"Hold up, hold up. I got you."

Rushing to her aid, I helped her from bed and into the master bathroom. Thankful that I'd never cleaned her shit out of my house or brought it to her, I grabbed one of the little black bands she used when it was time to suck my dick.

"Sosa, I love you," she confessed while on her knees and hugging the toilet. Gagging, she continued confessing. "I do. Do you believe me? I just want you to trust me."

"Yes, baby." I softened, being exactly who she needed me to be when she needed me to be.

"Do you trust me?" The words spewed from her mouth, followed by the day's meal. "Oh my God."

For the next five minutes, the only sounds present were those of her gagging and emptying the contents of her stomach. Once I felt like she'd gotten that shit out of her system, I carried her to the bed. She was still singing in my ear, but I'd partially tuned her out upon hearing her phone ring. The way that I was feeling, I prayed it was a nigga she'd given her digits too. It would be nothing to forward a number to my mans and have an address within seconds.

I grabbed it from the pillow beside her and noticed an unknown number was trying to reach her as well. Not thinking twice, I answered to see who it was. The same operator I'd heard minutes ago came blaring through the line.

"You have a collect call from..." Silence. "Brielle Jones."

Click.

My thoughts ran rapidly, forcing me onto the bed to process them. There was no coincidence that both Brielle and Cayman were both calling from jail on the same night. If my suspicions were correct—and I was certain that they were—then shit had gone south, and they'd both gotten popped.

The question was, why the fuck did Cayman feel comfortable with involving her in our operation? Drops were done alone. Period. No one was to know about them, and no one was to tag along. There was a small voice of reasoning in the back of my mind, telling me that he'd made the drop and got up with her later. Yet that logic didn't explain the fact that his burner had been answered and not by him. With him in custody, there was no way that he'd picked up.

"G." I shook her leg as the phone rang a second time.

"Hmmm." She stirred before falling back asleep.

"I need you to get up. Answer this phone. Someone is calling you."

"They can wait. It's probably just Brielle checking to see if I made it home."

"Was Brielle with you before you came here?"

"No. Unlike my man, hers picked her up from the airport. I rode home with Sauni."

"Her man?"

"Yes. Cayman. Baby, you should really take some notes from him."

"G, focus. What time did y'all flight land?"

"I don't know. About nine-thirty. We were delayed an hour in New York, but he waited on her."

"At the airport?"

"Yeah. I don't know. He was there when we got there because she'd already let him know when we'd land. We were just late."

"G, it's Brielle. She's gotten locked up." I had to do it. They were the only leads I had at the moment, and I needed to know all of the information they had.

"What?" Of course, she was all ears now. "When? How?"

If Cayman had been with her since nine, then she'd definitely made the drop with him. In fact, she'd even picked up the work with him. That shit made my blood boil. I answered the line and pressed the necessary digits for her to get through and put it on the loudspeaker.

"Mili." Brielle's voice came through muffled and strained. Certainly, she'd been crying.

"Brielle. What's going on? Why... Why are you in jail?" G raised from the bed.

"I... I don't know. We were on our way to the club. Neither of us knew that one of the bulbs were out in the taillight. Cayman got a call and said he needed to make two quick stops..."

Knowing that her calls were being recorded, I pressed the red button to disconnect the call. "Sosa. She was talking."

Too fucking much, I thought to myself. "It doesn't matter. She's coming home. Get dressed because you're going to get her. Have you sobered up?"

"I feel better now that I have thrown up."

"Good. We need to see what's going on and how we can get her home."

"Are you driving me?"

"I'm not going anywhere near a cell, love. I will be sending you to a special friend of mine. A bondsman. We're going to get this all settled."

GAUGE

No bond.

I couldn't believe that my best friend was sitting behind bars and could be for up to the next forty-eight hours. The list of charges that were tacked on to her jacket were appalling. After speaking with the bondsman that Sosa had sent me to, I learned that if convicted, Brielle would never see the light of day.

"I don't understand. What type of shit is Cayman into, Sosa?"

"You're asking the wrong questions. Your friend ain't no fool, G. Just like you know what type of nigga you're fucking with, she knows what type of nigga she's dealing with. This the type of shit that keeps reminding me of why you need to be as far away from me as possible."

"If something ever goes down, I'd put a bullet in a motherfucker's head before I let them haul you off to some fucking cell. Brielle ass don't belong there, but that's the price you pay for fucking with niggas like me. You still have a pass, G. Get out of this shit while you can."

"Quiet, Sos. I'm not going anywhere, and nothing

is going to happen. Let's just focus on getting Brielle and Cayman home, and we can worry about the rest later."

"They both coming home." I watched as Sosa walked out of the living room, fuming from the inside out. The smoke trailed behind him as he continued until he was no longer visible.

An incoming call from Sauni brought me back to life, but I quickly ignored the call. I was in no shape to talk, still feeling the effects of my hangover and not wanting to explain why our friend was behind bars.

With the way that I was feeling, nothing would calm my nerves like a hot shower and a nap. The sun was setting, and it felt as if the day had just faded before my eyes. I'd been a mess since getting the call from Brielle, hell even before then as well. My head was throbbing, and my eyes burned from the tears I cried due to frustration.

Not to mention that upon my return to Sosa's home, he was keeping up ruckus by yelling at the construction crew, demanding that they make more progress and faster. I had seen them each day since the second time I'd come over, yet I still didn't know what they hell they were building.

Sometimes, they would venture off into the house and be gone for hours. It wasn't always that everyone returned, which was even more confusing. But Sosa was making sure that I minded my business. According to him, I was such a freak that I'd invite one into his bed if he weren't on his job.

"Hey." I reached out to Sosa, who was staring blankly at the television in the bedroom.

It was watching him, because he surely wasn't watching it. The incarceration of his friend was really getting to him. I'd never seen him so anxious. He was the calmest person I'd ever encountered, so to see him rattled was complicated for me.

"Hey. Come shower with me."

"G, I really don't give a fuck about a shower right now."

"Well, too bad. Maybe it will calm you down." I pulled him up by the arms. "Plus, I've got a little surprise for you."

"I hate surprises. Tell me now."

"I was thinking that maybe I could use the bathroom mat to protect my knees from bruising on the tiles in the shower."

"Oh yeah?" His mood shifted, immediately.

"Mhmm. You still don't give a fuck about a shower?"

"Na, I don't, but I want to see what that mouth do though."

NINE

SOSA

"She's willing to cooperate."

Those words were like bombs sounding off in my head. They were the exact words that I didn't want to hear. Brielle would be released in a matter of hours along with Cayman. Gauge was on call to pick her up while the bondsman would be scooping Cayman. They'd been interrogated for the last seventy-two hours. While I knew that Cayman was tight-lipped, I had my suspicions about Brielle, and they had just been confirmed by Detective Lancer.

"What has she said so far?"

"She doesn't know much yet So, she only mentioned the basics. Where she's seen you. The fact that you're a friend of a friend. She was only with Mr. Uphill because she'd been out of town with friends, and they'd made plans to see one another that night."

"Did she give her friend's name?"

"No. Whoever her friend is, she's not giving us any name."

"Good. What are they offering her?"

"Immunity if she helps them take down both you and Cayman."

"And how do they suppose she do that?"

"Wiring. Audio. Video. Whatever evidence she can provide that will be helpful to our case. But they are going to be very specific and give her clues on what to ask, what to pay attention to, and what to be aware of. Half the damn informants don't have what it takes, but their involvement in suspects' lives gives them leverage that no one else has. With that, we can get damn near anything we want from them. Mention jail, and the shit goes downhill from there."

"Good looking out. I'll be in touch."

"I'll let you know if anything new arises."

"But as of right now, do you think they have enough to build a case against me?"

"Not unless Cayman gives a statement."

"Cool." That shit wasn't happening.

On the way to Gauge's house, I considered all of the possibilities to rectify this situation that Cayman had gotten us into, but each outcome was less than pleasurable. Either way, something would need to be done about the problem that had arisen, and it had to be done soon. The same dream had been replaying in my head for the last forty-eight hours, surely a fore-warning.

Instead of utilizing her driveway, I parked two blocks over and walked to her crib on foot. I wasn't taking any chances. Knowing that she was inside, I texted Gauge to let her know to unlock the back door for me. She stood by until I reached the threshold and pulled me into her arms the minute I was inside. Gauge had to be the mushiest motherfucker I knew, but I was down with whatever when it came to her. She knew that shit and used it against me every chance she got.

"I called you."

Since the incident, we hadn't separated, so Gauge had no clue that I had a new phone number. I figured now was the time to tell her. "I got a new phone."

"Oh, okay. Is it the number you texted me on?"

"Yeah. That's it. Have you talked to Brielle?" We moved through the house.

"Yes. She is being released. In a bit, I'll be heading down to get her. Are you picking up Cayman?"

"He's been released. I just got word on the way over here. He'll be through in a few if you don't mind."

"No, of course not. Maybe we can all get to the bottom of this."

We don't have to get to the bottom of shit. I know what went down. Instead of responding, I took my seat on the sectional and grabbed the remote control. It was time to play the waiting game.

"I'll be back in a bit. You going to be fine?"

"Yeah." She didn't have to worry about me. Her concerns were misplaced. Brielle was the bigger issue. I watched as Gauge gathered her things before walking out of the door. She'd assured me that she'd lock up, so I stayed put.

GAUGE

Tears flooded my eyes as I watched Brielle saunter over to my car. "Sauni! Here she comes."

In an instant, Sauni was out of the car and had run around to where I stood. Brielle looked nothing like herself; she seemed to have lost a few pounds, there were dark circles around her eyes, and her clothing seemed to be falling off of her.

"Brielle," I sang, expanding my arms and depleting the space between us two.

I couldn't stand the thought of being away from her a second longer. The anxiety was killing me. As soon as we touched, she broke down in tears.

"It is okay, love." Sauni rubbed her heaving back.

"I should've never left from with y'all," she wept. "I can't believe I've spent the last seventy-two hours in that hellhole. They treated me like shit."

"We're here now," Sauni assured her.

After not hearing from Brielle for two whole days, Sauni grew extremely worried. She'd gone by her house and called her phone a million times. It wasn't until her husband suggested checking the public records online did she find out that Brielle was incarcerated. When she called, screaming, I felt like shit for keeping the secret. However, I felt like Brielle would be out sooner and wanted to give her the chance to tell Sauni herself.

"Come on. Let's get you out of here."

We all crowded in Brielle's one-bedroom apartment and helped her wind down. When she emerged from the bathroom after a shower and clothing change, she resembled the woman that I had known all my life.

"I'm done fucking with thugs. If he ain't a square, then he can't rock with me. I can't be no one's trap queen... ride or die... down ass bitch, none of that. Fuck that. A bitch is facing big boy charges, and all I wanted was to see some strippers shake their ass and slide down the dick that they made hard. Now they trying to have a bitch sucking pussy for the rest of her life."

I couldn't contain my laughter, and neither could Sauni. Brielle was too much for anyone to handle. "Mili. I need to get home to my babies. Sorry to break up the party."

"It's all good. The last thing I want to do is be cooped up in the house, dealing with my thoughts. Mili, you mind taking me to the liquor store?"

"Not at all if you don't mind swinging by my house with me once we drop Sauni off."

"I don't. Let me get on some shoes."

Brielle had dressed herself in some cotton shorts and an oversized tee. When she returned from getting her shoes, they happened to be some fuzzy slides that brought life to her simple fit. Because her face was clear of makeup, she chose a pair of dark shades to cover her swollen eyes. It seemed as if she'd cried the entire three days she'd been away. I didn't blame her. Hell, I would've cried for at least two.

We piled in the car before making the journey across town to Sauni's spot. It was closest to my house with a liquor store just two blocks away. Once we were alone—Brielle and me—my concerns began stirring in the pit of my stomach, encouraging me to speak up.

"Are you okay?" I asked, lowering the volume to the music.

"I don't... I don't know, Mili." Brielle's voice splintered, displaying a full range of emotions. "I just... I should've followed my gut. Something kept telling me that something wasn't right. All day. I'd thought it was the early flight we took days before we were to depart, but when we made it safe and sound, I figured everything was good. I thought the feeling would eventually go away, but it didn't. When I sat my ass in that car with Cayman, it was even more intense. I should've known something wasn't right when we switched cars. I don't understand what he was thinking."

"He wasn't. He just missed you. That's all."

"Missed me? We're in the same fucking city, Mili. He could've handled his business and got up with me. I would've waited on him. I slept on that long ass plane ride. I would've been up. Now, I'm facing real fucking charges. I'm not giving up my freedom for a nigga that ain't even mine."

"You won't have to. Sosa will figure something out."

Brielle grew quiet before facing the window and shaking her head. There was an extended period of silence before she returned to me. "I just... I've got a bad feeling about all of this. Like, I just stepped into some shit that I won't be able to talk my way out of, ya know. Like I've finally up and done it this time. This shit is serious, Mili."

"I know, and we will figure it all out. Just stay positive."

"I'm trying."

———

SOSA

Gauge had been gone for all of two hours before I heard her car in the driveway. As expected, Brielle was tagging alone. I was still waiting for Cayman to show face, but I wasn't sure how the two would react to one another after everything had gone down.

Frankly, I wanted to chat with Brielle to see exactly what had gone down. With Cayman knowing that he'd fucked up, he'd try to make his story sound as reasonable as possible. Yet the truth was that there was no logical explanation to explain his bullshit.

"Hey, I brought back something for you to eat. I figured you'd gotten hungry."

I was famished and hadn't noticed the rumbling in my stomach until Gauge was fanning the Popeye's bag across my face. "What's good, Brielle?" I addressed her best friend. "You aight?"

Obviously appalled at the concern I displayed, Brielle was hesitant to respond, so I continued probing her. "They didn't give you too much of a hard time, did they? My lawyer is on call and can have..."

"No. Just was ready to get out of there." Brielle's demeanor had been altered. She wasn't the same obnoxious chick I'd met at the bowling alley; neither was she the loud mouth that I'd encountered at the diner. Something had broken within her, broken her spirit. Humbled her.

It was usually the reaction of many people who were tossed into the system for the first time and didn't know what to expect from that point on. I'd seen it hundreds of times before. It was no secret that the government wanted to swallow us as a whole, lock us up, or kill us dead in the street. Either was satisfying to them.

"So what they talking about?" Gauge busied herself in the kitchen as I began pulling the food from my bag.

"Said I'm in way over my head. Apparently, this is

much bigger than me. I don't have a clue what that means."

"They ask you any questions?"

"So many questions that I didn't have the answers to." That practically meant she'd give them answers if she had them. Strike one.

"Yeah. Can't answer what you don't know shit about."

"Exactly. I didn't want to frighten Mili, but they mentioned your name."

I was all ears. "They always mentioning my name." I shrugged as if her words were common, but they weren't. It wasn't until last year when two niggas on my team got popped that I got on the fed radar.

"And showed me pictures. Asked if I knew you."

"And..." I wanted to know more.

"I told them you'd been interested in my friend, but I never said who. I just want to keep Gauge as far away from this as possible."

Well, too bad. You just dragged her into this shit, dumb rat. I could feel my insides churning with each word she spoke. Strike two.

Gauge had nothing to do with what was going on, and Brielle should've simply said that she didn't know who the fuck I was. Truthfully, she'd only seen me in common spaces. That didn't mean she knew me, because she didn't. That should've been her answer.

Seeing as how discomforted and nervous she was, I knew that she'd fold at the mention of jail time. She wouldn't be able to do another day in that bitch. *Strike three.*

"Yeah. Just like you, she has absolutely no involvement in whatever bullshit case they're attempting to build. The pictures you saw, were they random pictures? Pictures I'd taken of myself?"

"I don't know. You know cops are resourceful and can scoop pictures from anywhere. Social media, the..."

"I don't do social media."

"Oh, well these were taken by someone else then. Now that I think about it, they were all off-guard pictures, so I doubt if you took them or had someone to take them."

"So what happened that night?"

I listened as Brielle narrated their night, play by play. From the sound of it, Cayman was pussy whipped and was making careless ass decisions just to keep her around. What was wild was ole girl didn't show an ounce of love for Cayman.

Clearly, she was pissed the fuck off and had every right to be. It was obvious that she'd toss his ass to the wolves if it meant saving her own life. The only bitch down to ride for a nigga was one that was in love. Her loyalty wasn't with Cayman, because he was just something to do for the time being.

As she concluded the story, Cayman began knocking on the door. "I got it."

Gauge had joined us and volunteered to get the door. "It's Cayman. You okay with seeing him?"

"Not really. I'm going to head to your guest room if you don't mind, Mili. Can you guys refrain from letting him know that I am here?"

"Sure."

"Matter of fact, I'll take this shit outside. Lock up behind me, and I'll see you tonight." I kissed Gauge's cheek and stood to stretch my legs.

"Okay. Once I get Brielle settled in, I'll be over." Gauge stood on the tips of her toes and pecked my lips.

"Aight."

When I made it to the porch, Cayman was ending a call. "What's up, Caym?"

"Man, shit. Shit all bad on my end."

"I've noticed. Care to tell me why you felt the need to jeopardize our operation? A taillight? Did you forget to inspect the bucket?"

"Man, it was so much shit going on. Brielle had called me in the middle of the drop. She was stranded at the airport and needed a ride." *Lies.*

"That's why the fuck they created Uber and shit like that."

"She left the keys to her crib back in New York, and I've got her spare."

Lies. The girl that I'd spoken to a few minutes ago would never give Cayman a key. She made it obvious they were just kicking it. He didn't have access to her twenty-four hours.

We stepped off the porch and onto the walkway. I remained silent until we were near his car. Before speaking, I took a look up at the house and then returned my gaze to Cayman. The shit that I was about to say, I needed him to hear clearly.

"She's going to talk."

"Na, I doubt that. We can get her out of this situation, Sosa. She's innocent, man."

"She's willing to talk. She's going to cooperate, Caym."

"Fuck!" he spewed, well aware of the consequences of a snitch.

"You need to get rid of her."

"Sosa." He bit his lip, pain present in his stance.

"Tonight."

Patting him on the shoulder after ordering him to murk the woman he had sprouted feelings for, I headed toward the back of the house for my car. There was nothing left to be said. Cayman had made the mess, so it was Cayman that would need to clean it up.

I wasn't remorseful of my decision, but I hated an innocent woman had been caught in the crossfire. To make matters worse, it was my girl's best friend. But that was the way the game worked. People were in and out of your life. It was a constant revolving door. As I continued walking to my car, I was reminded of why I wanted Gauge as far away from me as possible. Niggas were ruthless and willing to go to extreme measures to solidify their presence amongst the living and freedom while living. I was one of them.

TEN

GAUGE

3:48 a.m.

I couldn't understand why my cell was ringing for the second time in the last few seconds. I'd let the first call go to voicemail after checking the clock on the nightstand, but I considered the incoming. The number displayed across the screen wasn't familiar, and neither was it saved to my contacts.

"Hello."

"Mili, baby." The voice wasn't one that I recognized right away, but the distress it presented caused me to respond.

"Yes?"

"She's gone." There were tears, definitely tears. Many of them.

I wasn't sure whom was gone or whom I was

sympathizing with on my other line, but I was brought to tears as well. "Who's gone?"

"My baby. My baby is gone. Brielle is gone."

Snapping, I immediately recognized the long-distance number and voice as Brielle's mother. My movements caused Sosa to stir in his sleep. He'd finally been able to get some decent rest since everything had gone south the other day.

"What do you mean she's gone? I just dropped her off at home a few hours ago. Try her cell." By now, I was up on my feet, pacing back and forth across the wooden floors of the bedroom.

"She shot herself in the head, baby!" her mother wailed.

"She what?"

"G, everything good?" Sosa still had sleep in his voice.

"She's gone! My baby killed herself!" Mrs. Jones was hysterical on the other end.

Even worse than her own cries, the belting of Brielle's father in the background made the hairs on the back of my neck stand straight up. This wasn't happening. This couldn't be happening. The thought of my best friend taking her life away had me utterly perplexed and damn near numb. But in my numbness, I could still feel the pain.

"She's gone," I repeated, letting the words resonate.

My heart dislodged from my chest and fell onto the ground before me. I felt as if my world had come tumbling down as I heard Sosa calling my name and the thudding of my head. At that moment, darkness consumed me. The moonlight of the night wasn't prominent enough to contain it. It covered me whole.

"G!" Sosa's voice paired with cold water helped steer me toward consciousness. "Wake the fuck up, G." More water. "G! Come on, baby girl." More water. The sound of the shower became apparent, but Sosa's voice was still muffled. "Wake up," he continued calling out to me.

My lids were heavy, but I managed to spread them both with the bit of strength that I maintained. Sosa was standing over me, still yelling my name and sinking his fingers into my cheeks while shaking my head from side to side.

"Ummmmm." I groaned. The excruciating headache caused me to close my eyes again.

"Don't do that. Don't close your eyes. Fight that shit. Wake up, G," he coached.

"What happened?" I managed to get out.

"You collapsed. You aight? How you feel?"

"Like I've been hit by a truck," I admitted, eyes still closed.

"You gon' be aight. Let me get you out of this fucking shower."

I felt my body being lifted into the air before feeling the softness of thick cloth covering me. Sosa was wiping me down with a towel when I reopened my eyes. After I was completely dried, he began massaging my body with the natural oils that I kept on the dresser.

"Sos."

"Yeah, baby girl?"

As he kneaded the kinks from my body, my memory was triggered. I'd collapsed after being informed that Brielle had shot herself in the head. Remaining still and allowing Sosa to continue moisturizing my skin, I began to weep. My chest heaved, and my body trembled. The sound of Brielle's father screaming could be heard in the distance. Her mother's cries were the closest.

"Is she really gone?" I questioned.

"G."

"Tell me. Is she really gone?"

"I think that you should answer your phone. It's Sauni calling."

His massaging ceased as he handed me my cell, which I hadn't heard ringing. He'd already answered when he placed it up to my ear for me to hold. Neither of us said anything. Sauni's sniffles confirmed my suspicions. She knew. For all of two minutes, we shared the silence, no one knowing what to say or how to say it.

"Mili." Sauni was the first to break. I followed thereafter, succumbing to the battle with my emotions.

"I knooooow," was my only response. "I knooooow!"

"I have to go see this for myself. I won't believe it's

153

real until I see it for myself. She... She was just... with us," Sauni explained.

"I'm... I'm coming too."

Though I'd spoken the words, I was immobile. Paralysis had locked my legs and chained my arms to the bed. I was confined by invisible shackles that wouldn't let me move.

"I'll come get you then," Sauni offered. I was more than thankful for her generosity.

"I'm not at home. I'll meet you there."

At that point, I was freed from the chains and able to lift from the bed. Sosa continued to watch me from the edge with concern apparent by the look on his handsome face. I wiped my face, but it seemed as if I only made room for a fresh set of tears.

Sauni and I were still holding the phone, not wanting to end the call. Sosa sprang into action once he realized I was getting up. Like the hero he was, he saved the day by dressing me while I tried getting myself prepared for the drive back into the city. Carrying on as I was, I wouldn't make it past the driveway.

YELLOW TAPE.
Red blood.
Blue lights.
Black gun.

Rocking back and forth, I recalled the scene at Brielle's apartment.

Yellow tape.

Red blood.

Blue lights.

Black gun.

We'd been in the same place hours prior, and nothing was out of the ordinary. Now, my girl's home was a crime scene.

Yellow tape.

Red blood.

Blue lights.

Black gun.

"I love you," Sauni had cried in my arms. "Don't ever leave me," She begged, but she didn't have to worry. I wasn't going anywhere. As we watched the homicide detectives coming in and out of Brielle's apartment, we stood off to the side, holding one another.

Yellow tape.

Red blood.

Blue lights.

Black gun.

Nothing felt real, and everything moved in slow motion. I felt as if I were trapped in a nightmare, and no one would let me out. Both of our bodies trembled as we stared at nothing in particular, both attempting to come to terms with the fact that our friend had committed suicide. We were unaware that Brielle ever owned a gun, so this was appalling to us.

We were both asked a few questions while on the scene but nothing out of the ordinary. Detectives wanted to know when the last time Brielle had made contact, if she was under any stress, and had she ever attempted suicide before.

Yellow tape.

Red blood.

Blue lights.

Black gun.

"G, you have to eat this."

Sosa had been forcing food down my throat for the last forty-eight hours. That's how long it had been since I discovered my best friend had left me on this earth to suffer without her. I missed her more than she'd ever imagine. The loudness. The bluntness. The humor. The theatrics. I'd give my left lung just to have it all back.

"I'm not hungry."

It had been the same line I'd quoted and seemed to be all that I knew. Sosa had been accommodating despite my mental checkout. My physical was far behind because I felt like giving up every few hours when the pain would hit me all again.

Yellow tape.

Red blood.

Blue lights.

Black gun.

There was so much blood. We'd stayed until the scene was cleared, and we entered the apartment after police had vacated. She'd pulled the trigger in her bedroom, sitting on her bed. The walls were covered with brain matter and blood. Splattered and unevenly distributed on the nightstand, headboard, and floor. She'd done a number on herself.

Yellow tape.

Red blood.

Blue lights.

Black gun.

"I'm not leaving you alone until you take a bite, G. It's been two days."

"And I knew her for a lifetime, Sos!" I flipped.

"I know. I'm sure she'd make ya ass eat too. Even get on you about possibly getting skinny and fading away if you don't," a still patient Sosa retorted.

He was right. She would. A smile—one that I hadn't seen since getting that call—stained my lips. "I miss her so much." I tried holding back the tears. My eyes were sore to the touch. The pain had numbed me mentally, but I was physically aware and sensible.

"I know. Eat this shit and let me get you out of the house."

"Can we go buy her a dress? Sauni is getting her shoes."

"We can go buy whatever you want, baby."

"Thank you."

"Thank me by eating this food. It is only a burger

157

and some fries. If you're not feeling it, we can stop and get you something on the way to the mall."

SOSA

I despised the mall, but I was willing to put that aside if it meant getting G out of the house. While I didn't feel the least bit remorseful for Brielle's death, I hated the toll it had taken on my baby. I felt guilty of her pain when it was truly Cayman who needed to be carrying the weight on his fucking back.

Much like the girls, he was having a hard time dealing with Brielle's sudden death as well. We'd talked once since the shit went down, and that was only for him to confirm the deed had been done, which was just before I laid down to rest beside Gauge the night she got the call.

Leaving no trace was our signature, but we'd made exceptions. No matter what, I wanted to give Gauge and Sauni the closure they deserved without bringing attention to ourselves or stressing them out with Brielle simply disappearing.

Suicide was more plausible. Brielle had just come from jail where she was poked and primed to become a first-class informant. It was easier to believe that she'd gotten in way over her head and decided to take herself out of the misery awaiting her than to believe that she'd simply vanished into thin air. Because no body would ever be recovered. Not ever.

"You like this one?" Gauge held up a black jumpsuit with the sleeves caped.

"I thought you said you were getting her a dress?"

"I did, but something is telling me she'd prefer this. Brielle wasn't ashamed of that body of hers and flaunted it every chance she got. I think this is more her style."

"Fuck it then. Let's go with that."

To be honest, we could've came out the bitch with a swimsuit, and I wouldn't have given a damn. I'd been ready to roll since we stepped foot inside. The fact that we were near the finish line was gratifying.

We headed for the register as Gauge began telling me what she had come to expect for Brielle's funeral. "But with her parents planning everything, I don't know how much of it I can actually make happen."

"Baby, you fucking with a nigga with unlimited funds. If you want that shit, then that's what you're getting. Money isn't an issue. Besides, you have enough money stashed at your crib to pay for seven funerals."

"Sos." She squinted.

"I'm just reminding you, G. As a matter of fact, call her moms up and let her know to put everything on my tab. I want to make sure everyone is happy."

It was the least I could do after my people had ran up on her and forced her to hold the gun they'd put to her head before blowing her brains out. I honestly hated shit had to go down the way it did, but there was no room for informants in my world. If I ever discovered Gauge was on the same bullshit, I wouldn't hesitate to put her out of her misery.

That was the difference between Cayman and me. I could never lose sight of things. Pussy was good, and falling in love was an experience in itself, but that shit wasn't enough to taint my morals or risk everything I'd worked hard to accomplish. Shit was never that deep. Not for me, and I loved Gauge's dirty draws.

"You kidding, right?"

"Na, anything to see you smile again."

"Sosa, thank you so much. You don't know how much this means to me."

We concluded our trip with a few scoops of ice cream and some chocolate-covered strawberries that Gauge just had to have. Admittedly, they were good. I'd never tried them before. On the way home, we shared a comfortable silence and allowed the music to fill the space that our words didn't.

When we made it home, I bathed Gauge from head to toe before blowing her back out in the shower. She hadn't been to sleep in almost three nights, and I'd be damned if I let her make it a forth. I rubbed her body down with lotion and oil as I watched her fall asleep naked on the bed. She was the most precious thing to me. I watched for at least an hour before pulling myself from the bed and dressing to make a run. Waking her crossed my mind, but I was too afraid that she wouldn't find sleep again, so I opted to leave without informing her of my departure. Prayerfully, I'd return before she woke to drain her bladder as she did every morning around four.

When I made it downstairs, I checked the progress that was being made by Julio and his team. "Julio."

"Boss man. Everything is good for now, but I'm not sure how much longer."

"This is the calm before the storm. I can feel it. Give me at least an estimate, Julio. I need something."

"Eh. Another week, boss man. We have at least another week."

"Aight. Julio?"

"Boss man."

"A week."

"A week." Julio nodded.

"Be mindful that G is upstairs sleeping. Don't let none of these motherfuckers out of your sight."

"Got you, boss man."

ELEVEN

GAUGE

Is my living in vain?
Is my giving in vain?
Is my singing in vain?
Is my praying in vain?
No, of course not.
It's not all in vain,
Because up the road is eternal gain.

Although Brielle's parents had chosen cremation due to the fact that they lived over 1,000 miles away and wouldn't be able to visit their daughter's gravesite as often as they'd like, her homegoing was nothing short of amazing. I tried blocking the mental restrictions I had for their choice and focused on the beauty of the service.

The three women who were currently singing without the assistance of instruments sent chills up my spine. Even in the highly lit vicinity, there was a dark cloud crowding us all. The eulogy had been delivered, and our departure was near. However, I didn't want to move. Leaving my friend behind would bring me a great deal of sadness, even more than I'd encountered in the last six days leading to her funeral.

It was beautiful. Sosa had kept his word and spared no expense. I'd been sure to cover every base and made sure that my girl was sent out like the amazing being that she was. I still couldn't believe she was gone and found myself dialing her number every other day just to see if she'd pick up for me.

My throat was raw, and my face was swollen. I felt like shit, and I couldn't help but wonder just how long this pain would last. It was too excruciating to consider living with it for the duration of life. I wanted her back. I needed her back. It was as simple as that. Not having her would drive me insane.

"Baby, we have to get up." Sosa nudged me.

I realized the casket was being carried down the aisle, and it was time for the family to begin clearing. We were on the front row and due to head out first. But I couldn't move. I was stuck.

"She's coming with me," I wept.

"G, baby. She's gone, love. She's in good hands. I promise." He leaned over and whispered in my ear. "Come on."

"I can't. I can't do this, Sos."

"You can, and you will. I know it hurts, but you've got to keep pushing."

"Why?"

Sosa leaned forward and wiped my tears before standing and pulling me to my feet. "Because I'm not giving you another choice," he stated.

With his assistance, I slowly made my way into the aisle as associates, old classmates, friends, and people who Brielle knew from around the way gave their condolences to Sauni and me. My world was so damn dark without my sunshine. Brielle was the light of our friendship, and the gaping hole that she'd left was one that would never be able to be filled. That tore me up inside and made me wish that I'd stayed with her a bit longer and made sure that she was okay. Hell, I could've stayed the night with her or even at my own house while we shared the guest room.

There were so many what ifs and fingers I was pointing at myself, but I had to keep being reminded that Brielle was a determined being. I couldn't stay close to her side every hour of the day. If she had been having those thoughts, then she'd probably fall through on them and never mention them to me, as she hadn't. It was all still foggy and one big mystery, but there was one thing that I was certain of, and that was the lone fact that I wished I could've done more to prevent this.

Outside of the memorial, we were bombarded with people all trying to give hugs, and I simply wasn't feeling any of the attention I was receiving. "Baby." I nudged Sosa.

"Yeah?"

I wasn't aware of how many mutual associates we had until I saw them either gawking or making a dash to speak to Sosa, who seamlessly ignored them all. His attention was locked and loaded on one individual. Gauge Miliani Morrison.

"I need to get out of here." It was beginning to be too much, and my solitude was the only place I found an ounce of piece. "Where's Sauni?"

"She's talking to Brielle's parents. Would you like to say goodbye?"

"No. She'll understand. I need to get out of here."

"Okay. The repast is—"

"I can't be around all of those people, Sosa. Sauni isn't going either. We're having our own gathering. Just the two of us."

"Say no more." He nodded, and we set out for his car.

On the walk over, I noticed Cayman a few feet away. He was notably sad, head hanging and body sluggish. His street clothes had been swapped for a nice dark suit. His hair had been freshly trimmed around the sides, and his curly top was rather fluffy.

"Baby, there's Cayman."

"I see him," Sosa replied, but we continued without slowing the pace.

I'd at least expected him to address Cayman's presence, but I knew that wouldn't be happening by the time we made it to the car. Once inside, I pulled off my heels and reclined the seat. Exhaustion was wearing me down and had been for the past few days. Brielle's passing was so much to digest, and I still hadn't stomached it yet. I felt like at any time, she would come yelling and declaring her presence in the world.

"Buckle up." Sosa reached over and placed a hand on my thigh. He gripped the wheel with the other, and we pulled out into traffic.

SOSA

Gauge and Sauni had decided to celebrate the life of their friend at Gauge's place. Before leaving and heading to meet Detective Lancer, I made sure that they were both good. I'd gotten food catered at the last minute, a shitload of alcohol, a box of Kleenex each, and a fresh batch of DVDs. It was no secret what their plans were. They wanted to be alone in a judgment-free zone so that they'd have the freedom to cry their pretty eyes out.

I promised I'd return for Gauge and take Sauni to the crib if it was too late for her husband and kids to come scoop her. She'd been advised against driving herself because she would be in no shape to get herself back home.

As I tightened the hoodie around my head and

secured the shades on my face, I prayed that I heard some good news for once. To hear that Brielle's death would splinter their case would've been good. Shit, even the thought of them dropping the case altogether would satisfy me, but I was aware that it was highly unlikely.

In the travel shop, there were tons of people crowding the store and shopping for gas and other travel necessities that made a road trip more intriguing than the idea itself. It was a great distraction from the encounters I'd been having with Detective Lancer the past few weeks.

The seat behind him was occupied, and there were none available around him. Instead of taking the booth three rows back, I decided to order a meal and let the rest work itself out. As Lancer noticed me taking my place in the long line, he did the same. He was a rather small man, short and just as dark as me.

While he'd been digging up dirt on everyone involved with my case, I'd been snooping around his front door as well. Besides gambling debt, he happened to be clean. He'd been on the force for over ten years and was making strides and receiving promotions left and right. He was a hardworking dude.

"Anything new?" I began.

"Yeah." Lancer was regretful in his response.

"Shit, I thought their only new lead was Brielle."

"It was. They had plans to use her as bait. But they've caught a bigger pun now."

"Someone else willing to turn state?" I couldn't contain the rearranging of my facial expression.

This was news to me. I couldn't think of a bigger player. My operation was solid, and everybody was eating good. No one had a reason to fold. Even niggas who had taken losses and been imprisoned, I had their sentences reduced to mere months, and their families were good as long as I had breath in my body. No stone had been left unturned.

"Yes. Someone who is facing real time, someone on your team."

"Everyone on my team is free, and if I can help it, it's going to stay that way. I look out for mine."

"Well, this one is not too thrilled with the death of his girlfriend."

"Cayman?" Life flashed before my eyes. The brink of death seemed more tangible than ever now.

"Cayman." Lancer nodded. "I gave him my card to call me in case he ever decided he wanted full immunity—as we offered him—to give up everything he knew about you and your operation. He was livid that we would even consider him to be a snitch. Neither of us thought we'd get anything out of him."

"Until Brielle..." Defeat weighed heavy on my heart.

"Until his girlfriend committed suicide." Not even Lancer knew that I'd put the price tag on Brielle's head. "He called me this morning. I've never heard a grown man cry like that. It's really fucking with him, and I think he blames you."

"So what's the next step? Keep it one hundred with me."

"He's talking, Law." Lancer shook his head. "When I left the office an hour ago, he'd come in."

"How long do I have?" That was the most important question.

"I don't know."

"Come on, man. How long do I have?"

"He wasn't specific with his confession. It's still all hypothetical to us. We have to dig through his coded tongue and figure out what he meant by everything. He smelled like the liquor store. In an hour, we'd only gotten a few words out of him. I advised the team to return tomorrow to get a full confession because we weren't making good progress."

"So he's supposed to come back tomorrow?"

"First thing in the morning."

"Good looking."

I didn't get the burger I'd planned to order. My appetite had suddenly diminished. The thought of Cayman turning state because of a bitch that didn't give two shits about him and was prepared to throw him under the bus had me sick to my stomach. Immediately, I removed myself from the line and headed to my car. I needed time to consider what the fuck was going on and what needed to happen in order to redirect the situation and keep the odds in my favor.

With a confession from Cayman, my freedom would be stripped in a matter of minutes. He'd been with me since the start of this shit, my right-hand man. Him turning me over to the crackers just didn't seem logical.

"Fuck!" The steering wheel of the Honda caught a quick beating due to my raging temper.

I'd tried to fight it, the notable uneasiness in my stomach that felt much like I'd been bitten by the bug of betrayal, but it was apparent. My nigga was willing to rat me out. When I noticed his condition at the funeral, I knew some shit wasn't right. I felt it in my gut. He'd more than likely visited the nearest liquor store and drunk his sorrows away before calling Lancer to make a deal.

There was only one way to rectify this situation, and it wasn't through a conversation. If a nigga wanted to see me taken out of this bitch, then it would be in the afterlife because they wouldn't live to see my dismantling if I had anything to say about it. Friend or foe, anybody was welcome to feel my wrath. I grabbed my burner phone and dialed up Cayman's cell.

"Caym, you good?" His words were sluggish, but I could understand him clearly. It was obvious the alcohol was on his ass and not letting up.

"Man, I'll be aight. Bitches come and go every day, B."

He still wouldn't admit that he'd fallen in love with a woman who only wanted to have a good time. Now she was near ashes because of his foolish mistakes. If there was anyone to blame for Brielle's murder, it was him.

"Right. Where you at? I'm about to pull up on you. I need to rap with you about some shit."

"I'm chilling by the crib. Pull up."

I was definitely pulling up. When I ended the call with Cayman, I placed another to Andre, my top hitter. He would've taken the job if I'd offered it to him, but this was personal to me. I'd break his neck before I allowed him to lay hands on Cayman.

"Dre."

"What's good, Law?" Defiant by nature, he was one of the few niggas that referred to me by my last name.

"I need you to ready the potion. Warehouse. When you've gotten the shit together, you can leave."

"Ain't nobody going in? Where's the fun in that shit?"

He was ready to murk something, but I didn't have anything for him. Brielle was the last hit, and I prayed there wouldn't be more. I tried walking the straight and narrow, but some shit called for a bit of chaos. This happened to be one of those cases.

"This one is on me, fam. Just make sure that bitch cleared out after you get it together."

"Bet."

Cayman was surrounded by beer cans and liquor bottles when I arrived at his place. He was so far gone

171

that he had passed out on the couch by the time I let myself in with the spare key. From the looks of things, he'd been self-medicating since the death of Brielle. The rolled up hundred-dollar bill was a clear indication that Cayman was in way over his head.

He was derailing quick, and it pained me to even think that he'd stoop that low. Yet I couldn't deny the cocaine residue on his living room table. I now knew why he'd been talking out of the side of his neck and willing to fold. He was out of his mind.

"Caym!" I kicked his foot. "What the fuck you got going on in this bitch?" We lived like kings, not like peasants.

"Sosa." He stirred.

"Yeah, nigga, get up. Come take a ride with me so that I can run some shit by you. I'll have someone to come clean this shit up while we're gone."

"I'm good. I can clean this up myself. Ain't much. Where we going? To get up on some hoes?"

"I ain't free, Caym, and neither is my time. Fuck these hoes."

"Oh yeah, that's right. You passing up pussy 'cause you got in-house pussy."

"I'm passing up pussy because them bitches don't compare to my in-house pussy. Know the difference, nigga."

"She changing you, Sosa. Shit ain't a good look, dog."

"Only thing my bitch done changed about me is

the ice around my heart. I'm still the same nigga. It's you who let a bitch change you."

"I really fucked with her, dog."

"But she wasn't fucking with you, Caym. You were simply something to do because there was nothing else to do. Ole girl had just got through with her nigga, still getting over him. You in yo' feelings when ole girl ain't even have none. Not for you, nigga."

"You don't know what you're talking about, nigga."

"This shit came from her mouth."

"You never even had a conversation with her. You didn't like her from the jump."

"The fuck you mean? I ain't even ever gave the bitch enough thought to not like her. That was G's friend, not mine. Just as I wouldn't expect you to be all up in G's face, I wasn't all up in hers. Besides, the bitch talked too much for me. I like my hoes quiet."

"And that's why you wanted her dead."

"Damn real. Doesn't take a science degree to figure that shit out. Come on, nigga. I got some shit I gots to do."

"Aight, give me a minute."

"Na, come on, Cayman." I was tired of going back and forth, so I helped him to his feet before allowing him to lead the way out of the door. Thankfully, he could stand and walk. I didn't have time to wrestle with this nigga.

Cayman had passed out again twenty minutes into the ride. As I pulled up to the warehouse, I made sure it was vacant before waking Cayman from his sleep. It would've been easier to handle this shit while he was unaware of what was going on, but I wanted him alert. I wanted him to know why I had chosen to put him out of his misery so that he could go join Brielle wherever the fuck she was. I needed him to understand that any motherfucker could get it, no exceptions. If he was willing to take me under, then I was willing to take him down.

As I patted his cheek to wake him, his cell rang. I chastised myself for not making sure that he left it behind and made a promise to carry it back to his home before destroying it. I needed his final location to be his home if police ever went sniffing around his phone records. I'd called him from a burner that I destroyed after we hung up from one another, so there would be no traces of me in his incoming or outgoing calls. We hadn't talked in days.

"Unknown," I spoke aloud without realizing it. Though I couldn't see it, I could feel the scrunching of my face.

Just as I blazed, Cayman's cell phone rang. He frowned upon noticing that a restricted caller was attempting to reach him

"Watch out!" was all we heard through his speaker before the windows to my hummer shattered, and bullets rained through.

I dropped the blunt that was hanging from my mouth as the sound of the windows startled me. Before I could take cover, I felt myself losing consciousness. A burning sensation ripped through my body as I closed my eyes but not before the crimson blood leaked through my solid white tee.

"We out!" the assaulters yelled. Their deed had been done.

The dream I'd been having for months came rushing back. To make matters worse, I'd blazed two blunts to take my mind off of the shit that I was about to do. I needed to numb the feeling of betrayal that was weighing me down.

Forewarning. Though it wasn't spot on, the dream had so many references that all made sense now. What fucked with me the most was the fact that I ended up on the brink of death, and Mili ended up alone before I woke each time.

I ignored the call and continued waking Cayman. When he finally realized where we were, he became more alert. "Somebody gots to die tonight, huh?"

You, nigga, I wanted to say, but I'd save that shit for later.

"Sosa just going to kill everything walking. One bad motherfucker."

He was starting to get on my fucking nerve with his rambling. I was happy I didn't have to hear that shit in the car. It all felt strange, loving a nigga like your blood brother one minute and despising his ass the next. Cayman had quickly switched roles and become the enemy. Even though he looked the same, the nigga wasn't.

It was gruesome, watching him lead us both to his death. When we made it inside of the warehouse, him stumbling and me following closely behind, it became apparent what was about to go down. Cayman was drunk, but he wasn't a fool.

"Where the crew? Where the victim?"

"Right there." I pointed as he surveyed the building for signs of life besides us two. He wouldn't find any.

"Right where?"

"You, Cayman."

"Me?"

"Yeah, nigga. You."

"What you mean? Quit playing, dog."

"Since you want the bitch so bad and is willing to do anything to avenge her death, I'm going to send you to her. Hopefully, she'll have a change of heart and want you this time... knowing you were willing to turn state and die for her. You had to know this would be your fate. Right?"

"Sosa. Man, listen. It's not what you thinking..."

"Oh, I know it's not. What I thought was my nigga would never flip. Couldn't have paid me to believe that shit, but it's true."

"Na, that shit ain't true, dog."

While listening to him come up with insufficient lies, I removed the blunt from behind my ear and sparked it. Smoke filled my lungs, helping me manage the stress of knowing that I'd be responsible for the death of my homie. I'd tuned him out as flashbacks of us as boys became vivid in my mind. Never in a million years had I thought we'd get to this point.

"Caym," I interrupted him, knowing that Gauge was waiting, and Sauni would be needing a ride home because it had gotten so late. "Step inside of the barrel."

The blue barrel was filled to the brim with acid that would eat his flesh to the bone once inside. After the flesh was dissolved, the bones would follow. The process was a lengthy one, but I didn't have plans to stay for the duration. The acid was heated, which sped up the decomposition by hours, but I didn't have that kind of time. Dre would be back in twenty-four hours to dispose of the residue.

"Sosa, man."

"Cayman, you've been a gangster since I've known you. Don't go out like a pussy. Man the fuck up."

I was hesitant about upping my pistol, but when I realized he wouldn't go in without a fight, I aimed it at his head. "Cayman."

"That's what you're going to have to do, nigga. 'Cause I ain't getting in that bitch by myself."

"Your choice." I cocked back and put a bullet into each of his feet, which caused him to stumble backward and into the hot acid.

His cries were torturous as he tried fighting his way out of the barrel but was unsuccessful. Within seconds, the squeals had diminished to gurgling before complete silence. I preferred it.

After thirty minutes and another blunt, emotions were sneaking up on a nigga. The pain in my chest couldn't be denied, and neither could the tears welling in my eyes. I swiped them before they could fall and forbade any others to follow. My time had come, and my deed was done. As fucked up as it was, it was either him or me. I'd always chose myself over anyone else. That's how I'd made it this far, and I wasn't looking back.

When I arrived at Gauge's crib, Sauni wasn't there. I assumed her people had come for her. That was fine with me. Instead of waking Gauge, I tossed her over my shoulder and put her in the car once I'd used her key to lock the door. I showered before climbing in bed and wrapping her in my arms. It seemed as if the world around me was in chaos, and she was the only sure thing about it.

Honestly, I'd never expected to feel much of anything for a woman, but G was on some other shit. She didn't bring drama to a nigga's door, and she knew her place. She let me roam the streets and come back home to her when I was done. Shit kept my dick hard and my balls drained. Her head could put any nigga on his ass, and that pussy was one of a kind.

Just as I got comfortable, my cell began chirping. It was Julio, demanding my presence downstairs. When I made it to the sight of construction, he stood there with his hands on his hips. His team wasn't far behind him.

"Boss man, our job here is done."

"Everything is ready?"

"Everything is ready. Would you like to have a look?"

"Not tonight. I will revisit in the morning. Do you have the instructions for me?"

"Everything is inside. Maps. Instructions. Safe. Keys. Everything that you included in the plan."

"Good looking. Let me let you all out."

Julio rounded up the crew and headed toward the garage. It was their entry point. Every day, the same van reappeared with workers inside. They never carried a single tool or even made their presence known until inside of my garage, one that had been built specifically for them.

As we stepped into the garage, I noticed that it had been covered in sheets of plastic. "What's this?" I asked, watching Julio ready his weapon. "Julio," I commanded a response, but after I heard his chopper speak, there was nothing left to be said.

He swept across the room, laying down the fifteen workers that had been on staff since he'd been hired for the job. I shook my head, noting that the plastic was positioned so that no traces would be left behind. I thanked God that my bedroom was soundproof, or I'd have some fucking explaining to do when Gauge made it downstairs.

"I don't trust them, amigo."

"Fifteen niggas, Julio."

"None of them have wives. None of them have kids. I got them off of the streets and kept them housed until now. None of them have a clue what they're going to do after this. Half of them are addicts. For the right price, they'd fuck me over, as well as you. I can't have that on my conscious, amigo."

"Clean this shit up, Julio." I waved across the room.

Shit, I was ruthless, but this nigga was as savage as they came. In the last week, death had visited so many times that it was becoming normal. I didn't flinch at the site of the bodies in my garage, but that shit had me livid. Julio could've waited until he was out of my house.

"I plan to. I'll be out of your hair by the time the sun rises. It's been nice working with you, Sosa. Call me if you ever need anything. Anything."

"I won't hesitate," I assured him before heading back up the stairs.

I sealed my bedroom door before climbing back into bed and accessing the feed throughout my house. There were cameras everywhere. Julio would get his ass blown off before he could make it to my bedroom if he was feeling fishy, but I doubted it. However, with the amount of betrayal lurking as of late, everyone was suspect.

TWELVE

GAUGE

For three days, I'd awaken in the bathroom, hugging the toilet. This morning was nothing short of another disappointment where I was kneeled on the floor, emptying my guts. To make matters worst, I was thirty days late. With so much going on in the last few weeks—including the death of my best friend—I figured the stress had kept it from coming down.

"Mili!" Sauni yelled throughout the house.

I'd been home for a week. Sosa mentioned the fact that he had business to tend to and needed me to stay at my own place for a few. Since the day of Brielle's funeral three weeks ago, he'd been distant. According to him, shit was changing rapidly, and he was trying to get a hold on everything before it all slipped from his grasp.

"In here," I managed to get out before heaving and

spilling dry air into the toilet. There was nothing left inside of me.

Sauni rushed into the bathroom where I was. Her tiny feet plummeted on the wooden floors that were throughout my home. "Hey, love. Aww. I'm so sorry you don't feel good. I got you some soup, Ginger Ale, and a pregnancy test."

"Sauni. I don't need one. I'm pretty damn sure Sosa has succeeded in his mission. He's been shooting up my club since the second time we were intimate. I'm surprised it's just happening."

"Well, even if you already know, this is a keepsake. I have my pregnancy test from the girls still. It's in their scrapbook."

"How cute."

"Oh, someone woke up on the wrong side of the bed this morning."

"And for the last three mornings. I'm sorry, but I'm just tired of being so damn sick."

"It won't last forever, love."

"I guess I'll see soon enough."

"Have you talked to Sosa?"

"I haven't. Not in two days, which is highly unlikely. If he doesn't call me by tonight, I'm popping up."

"Well, Mili, you have to understand that he's going through a lot right now. Besides, it seems as if you need a little time too."

Sauni always had to be the voice of reasoning, but right now, I wanted her to be on my side. I was plain ole sick without Sosa and wanted her to understand it. The hard part about missing him so much was wondering if he missed me any. The attachment I'd developed for him was unhealthy, but most relationships thrived off of the attachment. So I wasn't sweating it. I loved my man, and it was that simple. A week was too long for anyone to go without seeing the one they loved.

"No. He needs to be right here, feeling the same pain I'm feeling, dealing with this damn demon child he's put inside of me."

"Don't say that!" Sauni chuckled. "My baby will be an angel. Watch!"

"Everybody is an angel to you, Sauni. Your opinion doesn't count."

"Well, that was just mean. Come on. Get up. I know you've got to pee."

"Seems as if this damn bladder is never empty."

"This is just the beginning. Wait until baby is big and sitting right on it. The worst!"

"You're not helping with my misery, Sauni."

"Then don't think of it as misery!"

"Give me your little test so that I can give it to you to scrapbook." We both chuckled as Sauni assisted me off of the floor.

"Sounds like someone is overly excited to be expecting."

"Yeah. You." I snatched the box and pulled down my pants.

"I don't think I want to be present for this part." Sauni tried running from the bathroom.

"Na, stay your happy-go-lucky ass right there." I nearly pissed myself, laughing. Sauni was tired of me already, and she'd just gotten here. "Seriously, don't leave. I may never take it. Not even acknowledge this when my stomach is too big for me to tie my shoes."

"Don't say that. You're going to be fine, Mili. Babies aren't the end of the world."

"I know. I'm just not ready to have one of my own," I admitted. "Hell, I'm not ready to share my man with some spoiled brat."

"Oh, that is the worse, honey, especially if you're having a girl."

"Exactly. Sosa will forget I even exist."

"Until it is time to feed or change diapers. Trust me. He will remember you then."

After I'd taken the test, we waited in the bathroom until the required two minutes had elapsed. As I'd figured, I was good and pregnant. Sauni was all smiles, while uncertainty poured in large quantities for me.

"Here. This is the second one. This one will tell us about how far along you are. You can dip it in the small cup that you used."

I followed the directions and waited the additional time to be greeted with the length of my pregnancy. Sosa crossed my mind, and I wondered if his reaction would be the same as mine. I also wondered how I would break the news to him.

Seven weeks.

"Sauni, seven weeks is a long time. I've been drinking. At least twice, maybe three times." I rested on the bathroom counter.

"And you'll be alright, Mili. Before I knew that I was pregnant, I was partying hard. Hell, that's how I got pregnant." Sauni took a seat on the toilet after letting the lid down.

I remembered, but that still didn't help me feel any better. "Still. Isn't that harmful to the baby?"

"Mili, I'm aware of every time you have had a drink. Trust me, you haven't harmed the baby. I'm going to put these two tests in some good plastic from your kitchen, and then we're going to decide on how we will tell Sosa that you're having a mini Sosa."

"I could always just tell him, you know." Shrugging, I decided that I'd force him to let me come over and give him the news after he gave me some dick. That sounded better than any plan that Sauni would be able to conjure.

"There's no fun in that. We need to make it special, something to remember."

"Oh, I've got plenty to remember, Sauni."

"Hush, simple child, and let's get you dressed. Staying in the house will only cause you to focus on the sickness, and it will consume you."

"Where are we going? I don't have to put on clothes, do I?"

"I mean, I would suggest it unless you're trying to catch a charge. Nudity—publicly—is against the law, honey."

"You know what I mean."

"In that case, no. Just get comfortable." Sauni stood and grabbed my hand.

She led me into the bedroom where we continued making light of my pregnancy and finding something suitable to wear wherever she was planning to take me. At this point, I had no objections. She was right. Being in the house led me to focus on nothing but my lack of wellness and overbearing sickness.

***

SOSA

The same place.
The same time.
Same hoodie.
Same shades.

Frankly, I was exhausted by the constant meetings that I had with Lancer. Each time I pulled out of the parking lot of the travel station, I was hit with another blow. First, it was Brielle. Then, it was Cayman. I could only wonder what I was in for this time. Lancer had been the one to request the meeting we were currently having.

"Lancer." I slid into the booth behind him.

"How's it going?"

"Everything is everything." I didn't give specifics; neither did I express the stress that I felt. Even the pain of Cayman's death was tucked away.

"I have some good news and some bad news."

"Hit me with the bad news first."

"They're ready to move in on you. Though they don't have much to go on, they want to get you downtown and shake you up. They're planning to pin conspiracy on you from the little chat they had with your buddy."

"Cayman."

"Yes. They've studied that audio day and night and have been trying to figure out what the fuck he's saying for two weeks. And the fact that he's gone missing is more ammunition."

"Do they have anything that can stick?"

"They can make some shit stick, Law. If they don't have anything, it isn't shit for it to be planted." He was correct. They wanted me worse than they wanted their next promotion.

"How long?"

"Seventy-two hours top."

"I need more time." Seventy-two hours wasn't shit. I still had work that needed to be done.

"That's all the time you have."

"Good news?" Shit, I'd heard enough bad shit for a lifetime.

"I finally got something on the lead detective in your case."

"Oh yeah?" That was surprising.

"Yeah, she's not so clean after all. She has some skeletons in her closet as well."

"Good looking."

"Check the toilet liner box in the second stall, and the file you need will be there."

"Aight. 'Preciate you." There was nothing left to be said.

"No problem. And Law?"

"Yeah?" I asked before standing.

"I suggest you run, man. Detective Shaw has it bad for you. She won't stop until she's taken you down."

"'Preciate that."

I planned to do just that. If they wanted me, they'd have to catch me. For the last two weeks, I'd been making plays and preparing my operation for my departure. Gauge had been forced to stay home for the past week because I needed a level head when securing my freedom and hers as well.

In these types of situations, you just never knew. I'd seen girls—Brielle being one of them—taken down even when they didn't have a clue about their man's dealings. I refused to let that shit go down with G. She was coming with me. Shit, we were both going to be on the run.

By the time I reached the city's limit, Gauge had called me three times. If I had to take a wild guess, she was calling to complain about the lack of time we'd been spending. It had been the same song all week, but I had shit to do. With everything I had going on, I needed her as far away from me as I could get her.

"What's good, G?"

"Don't *what's good* me, Sos. I'm coming over tonight, so get ready to open the door. I gave you a week. Whatever you don't have done will have to get done with me there."

She'd just turned my house into hers. I was scared to tell her ass to chill because I knew she'd come ASAP if I did. Gauge was turning me into a pile of fluff, and it bothered me on the daily. She was the only tender spot I'd ever possessed other than my mother.

"Who you talking to, G?"

"You!"

Of course she was. "Tone that shit down, or I'll make it another week. Don't sound like you miss a nigga anyway with all of that wolfing you're doing."

"Well, I do. Plus, I'm about to give this pussy to the next fine ass man I see. It can be the mailman for all I care. I'm horny."

"You ever had your neck broken?" I questioned.

"I wouldn't have lived to tell you if I had, Sosa."

"Exactly. Keep playing, and you won't live to tell the next motherfucker either."

"Where are you?" She softened.

"Handling business. I need you to chill, G. A lot is

going on right now. I ain't dodging you; I'm just working."

"I know. I just miss you. I'm coming over tonight, and I'm not taking no for an answer. I need some sex and some of your time."

"And you can have both, baby girl. Just let me finish what I'm doing, and I'll see you tonight. I'll be home around eight."

"I'll be there a minute after—8:01."

"I believe you too."

"Because you know I'm not lying."

"Catch you later, G."

I had to be the one to end the call. If she could, Gauge would hold the phone all damn day. She was spoiled rotten, and I was regretting making her that way. Now, the distance I needed to secure our future was causing a ruckus. She wasn't having that shit, really. In a way, it made me proud. I'd never had anyone as eager to simply be in my presence before. Not because of the money, status, or for gain; Gauge just wanted me. I could remove the millions of hats I wore each day, and that in itself was addictive.

True to my word, I made it to the house a little after seven. Knowing that Gauge was waiting to see me, I texted her to let her know that I had made it. I could imagine how fast she ran out of the house after receiving it.

She came bearing food, which made me a happy man. To my surprise, she'd cooked baked chicken, green beans, and mac and cheese. For desert, Gauge had baked a chocolate cake. Baby girl was definitely bored out of her mind. Since I'd been knowing her, she hadn't touched the stovetop. She was a hell of a baker, but I didn't consider that actual cooking. At least that's what my mother had told me as a kid.

"G, why you didn't tell me you knew how to cook?"

"Why would I want to slave over the stove when you're willing to have food catered or take me out to the finest diners where I can pig the hell out? That's doing too much." She chuckled. I missed that smile. I hadn't seen it in forever, or so it seemed.

"Good to know you only want a nigga because he feeds you good."

"Good dick and good food. Can't beat that, Sos."

"Can I give you this good dick in the morning, G? I'd be lying if I said I wasn't tired."

"Na, you can power up, take a nap or something. I'll be up waiting when you get up. I've had a nap already, so I'm up for a minute."

"Yes, ma'am," I replied sarcastically.

"Real funny, Sosa." Gauge rolled her eyes.

"I'm just saying. You really think you running shit, huh?"

"No. I just know that I have to remind you that you have a woman. You've went your whole life without worrying about a woman's needs, so it is my job to keep you on your toes."

"Whatever. I'm not taking your little behind to no

more restaurants. You can make yourself useful and get in this kitchen from now on. Let me remind you of your man's needs."

"Whatever you want, Sosa." Gauge cleared my plate and placed it in the sink.

"Is that you being nice so that you can have your way with me tonight?"

"You know me so well." She blushed, her cheeks reddening and eyes batting.

"Get ya ass up here, G. I'm tired. I give you permission to wake my ass up after eleven."

"I didn't need your permission, baby. That was the plan anyway."

I never told her I loved her, ever. Even when I expressed the love I had for her, I couldn't bring myself to tell her exactly how I felt. It was in the midst of my anger. But it was moments like this that made me want to remind her that I did. Because the words wouldn't flow from my mouth, I grabbed her by the neck and tongued her down instead.

"Come on, G."

We headed up the stairs where I shitted and showered as she watched, chatting away about her week without me, which sounded boring as shit. I understood why she was ready to see me. I was her entertainment. I gave her little ass something to do. By the time I was counting sheep, Gauge had succumbed to sleep as well. I guessed the nap she mentioned wasn't much to rely on.

"YES... BABY," Millie whined. She nearly wanted to cry. The crackling of her voice tugged at my heart-strings, ones that were solely attached to her and the being that would be birthed in a few short months.

Sleep had just overcome her, and I was waking her already. "I hate to wake you, but it's time for me to go." I rubbed her stomach in circular motions. The feeling was so soothing that it was coaching Millie right back into the slumber she'd been in. This wasn't helping much in my situation.

"You hear me, Mi?" I questioned, removing my hand from her stomach.

"Yes... baby," she repeated.

"Open your eyes."

Utterly helpless in the situation, I was tempted to let her be. But I knew that I'd be even more heavy-hearted if she wound up disappointed in my sudden departure. I wouldn't hear or feel the end of her wrath for weeks. As mellow as baby girl was, she had a fierce mean streak that I steered clear of at all costs, even if that meant waking her after finally finding comfort to rest.

"I can't." Millie groaned, a single tear falling from her right eye though she'd never opened it.

I was regretting even coming up to bother her, but I didn't want to hear the bickering later, so I did what I *thought necessary. "I ain't mean to wake you. Rest well, love. I'm out." I stood from the bed.*

With her eyes still closed, she replied, "I'm sorry. I'm just tired." Her whimpers were like daggers through my chest.

3:52am.

I clenched my pistol as I gained consciousness. It was after three in the morning when I arose again. Still, Gauge laid beside me, sound asleep. The dream I'd been having revisited me, waking me in the nick of time. The shit felt so real. I'd gained enough willpower to force myself awake before the craziness.

Taking a peek at my slumbering love, I contemplated waking her with a dose of good dick but decided against it. There were a few things I needed to do before climbing back in bed. When I did, it would be to wake her with my tongue. It had been a minute since I tasted her sweetness, and I wouldn't deprive myself any longer.

I tossed on a pair of basketball shorts and a T-shirt. The air conditioner didn't give a damn about me preferring to work in my boxers. When I reached my office, I flipped the light on and waited for it to illuminate the large space. It wasn't often that I visited my office. There were people in place to handle my dealings. But since I'd had a target on my back, I'd seen the mahogany desk and cushioned chair more than I had since building my home four years prior.

"Let's see what you got going on," I referred to Detective Shaw, who was over my case.

The folder I'd taken from the stall was small, not very significant in size, but I was hoping it packed a punch. Confusion settled within me as I surveyed the outdated photos of Detective Shaw. She looked to be no older than sixteen or seventeen with a stomach that protruded. It was obvious that she was pregnant, but I wasn't sure exactly what her pregnancy had to do with my investigation until I reached the final photo.

I hadn't formally met Gauge's father, but I had seen several pictures of him. I'd seen enough to know that it was him standing beside Detective Shaw with his hands caressing her stomach. It was obvious that they were young and in love. The first document in the file was a birth certificate, absent of the birth mother's name, yet Gregory Ellis Morrison was labeled as the biological father.

I could feel steam radiating from my nostrils and ears as my chest began to burn. I continued flipping and reading the documents that Lancer had gotten ahold of. According to his observation, Destiny Shaw and Gregory Ellis Morrison had given life to a baby girl, Gauge Miliani Morrison, as teenagers. Destiny Shaw signed over her parental rights in the hospital. His lead ran cold, so he couldn't exactly tell me what happened thereafter besides Gauge being raised by her father.

The final few pages were more recent photos.

There was one of Gauge's mother at her high school graduation. There was another of Gauge's mother at her college graduation. Lastly, there was one of Gauge and her mother standing side by side at Red Lobster in the dress that I'd purchased with the sparkly shit all over. It was the most recent.

Sick was an understatement. I felt deathly ill. Beads of sweat began surfacing on my forehead as my throat dried and head began to throb. This shit couldn't be true. I had been sleeping with the enemy.

Anger overcame me as I pulled back the top drawer of my desk and retrieved one of the many Glocks I had stored around my crib. As I stood from my desk, the loud siren rocked me to my core. There were silent triggers that would alert me if anyone stepped into my yard unannounced. It was the same alarm that Gauge had triggered the night she'd come to my house without warning me.

Immediately, I turned on the monitors in my office to see who was here to get their head blown from their shoulders. The sight before me wasn't one I'd grown to anticipate. My legs locked and heart pumped at the sight of armed federal agents crawling through my yard.

Springing into action, I ran into my bedroom and grabbed the single duffle that I'd need to carry with me. The sight of Gauge lying peacefully in my bed infuriated me. I couldn't fight the urge to put her to rest permanently. Cocking my hammer back, I marched to her side of the bed and put it to her dome.

She jumped from her sleep after feeling the pressure of my gun at the center of her head. "Sosa, what is going on?"

"I loved you!" I admitted, emotions becoming too much to bare. For years, I'd kept my heart on a leash, and the minute I gave it up, I was played like some fucking fool. My pride wouldn't let that shit go, not ever. So G had to go. The thought of it all caused an aching in my chest that couldn't be explained.

"Sosa! I love you too!"

"She's your mother. She sent you!"

"Who sent me?"

"Destiny Shaw."

"Sosa, what are you talking about?"

"She's after my freedom, and she sent you to help bring me in."

"No. My mother? I haven't talked to her in forever, Sosa. My father raised me. I didn't even have a clue that she was after you... that anyone was after you. I could've gotten this all worked out for you. For us."

The alarm continued blaring, but I heard every word she'd said. For some reason, I believed every one of them, but my trust had been altered. There was no way I could be sure if she was being honest.

Boom!

The sound of the agents trying to get through my door brought me back to reality. There was minimum time left for me to flee. I spared Gauge's life. I had to. There wasn't enough strength in me to pull the trigger. I'd bodied the toughest niggas, yet I couldn't bring myself to kill baby girl. A life without me would be worse than death for her. This, I knew.

"Sosa, come back!" she hollered as I backed away and ran out into the hallway.

I didn't worry about the stairs, deciding to jump over the banister to save myself time. Gauge's footsteps could be heard coming down the steps as she continued screaming my name.

"Come back to me!" she was adamant, catching up to me as I heard the windows to my home being shattered. "Come back to me!"

For an entire year, I'd been perfecting my emergency escape. The door that was within my reach would secure the moment I was inside and closed it. There wasn't any amount of force that would be able to reopen it. The door led to a thirty-mile-long tunnel, which would lead me to a secure location where a private jet would airlift me to my destination.

Julio and his crew had been slaving to make this possible. It was the final piece to the puzzle I'd created, one that the government wouldn't be able to solve with their smartest team members. It was a plan that once included Gauge, but it had been reduced to a one man's show again.

As I felt her tugging on my shirt, I realized it should've stayed that way. In the life that I lived, there was no room for love. There was no room for laws. There was no room for us.

"Come back, Sosa, please." Gauge was determined to slow me down, and she had.

While she continued pulling at my shirt, I spun around and lifted my arms one by one, maneuvering the duffle as I went to come up out of the shirt altogether. Gauge went plummeting to the ground with a loud thud.

"Sosa, no. Please, please don't do this."

I never responded, too afraid that I would need more than a few seconds to spew the venom I wanted to pump into her. I'd given her my most valuable possessions—money and time. Yet I was the one left looking foolish. It wasn't enough that I'd risked my sanity to fuck with her and keep her happy. She wanted my freedom too.

I'd need a lifetime to help her understand the hatred that I'd bred for her. There wasn't a person I hated more on earth, not even her fucking mother. She'd hadn't been the one to come into my life and make shit right. She'd didn't brighten my dark ass days. She didn't make me reconsider my train of thought. She hadn't made me alter my ways. She hadn't made me fall in love *lawlessly* and without shame.

That was all on Gauge, the sick motherfucker who didn't want to let me go even after she'd been caught. The damn girl was relentless, getting right back up after falling on her ass. But she wasn't quick enough.

By the time she reached me, there was an army of men and women behind her, yelling obscenities. Guns were drawn and ready to fire.

I'd opened the door and stepped inside as I heard the voice of a woman demanding that the officers lower their weapons. It was Destiny Shaw, a woman who'd rubbed off on her child even though she hadn't raised her. The two were the most relentless piece of shits that I'd ever encountered besides myself.

"Gauge," she spoke.

"You did this! Make him come back!" Gauge yelled.

She was closer. Close enough for me to smell the delicate fragrance she wore each day as I punched number after number into the keypad to seal the door.

"Please. Come back to me!" She yelled as the door began to close.

I didn't want to care. I didn't want to want her. I didn't want to feel sympathy. But I couldn't help myself. Her cries were torturous. Relief washed over me as the door met the opposite side of the tunnel. Freedom hadn't evaded me, but heartbreak had caught up to me.

"I'm pregnant!" Gauge bellowed in agony as I sealed the door behind me, causing my heart to stop.

To be continued...

AFTERWORD

A Mercy Message

There are a few fun facts that I would like for you to know about the inspiration of this story, the hero, and the heroine.

The meet up simply came from a real-life experience. A family member started a group text and happened to put someone in our message thread that didn't belong. While the entire family wanted the unknown member out of our group, I drew inspiration from their presence.

The heroine is every bit of me. While everyone is searching and wondering about what they want in life, I'm sure of myself, my potential, my preferences, and my intentions.

Our hero, Sosa, represents the misunderstood black men all over the world. In addition, he's confident in his position and is willing to go to the ends of Earth to maintain it. Give it some thought. His empire is all he has and all that he's ever loved. **Beyond the shadow of doubt, he's going to fight for what he loves.**

Be sure to leave your thoughts on this couple in the form of a **REVIEW** on Amazon. I'd love your feedback.

Until book two,

Mercy B

P.S. There is an AMAZING soundtrack dedicated to Sosa and Gauge—as well as the mood I was in while writing their love story. **CLICK HERE** to listen.

ABOUT THE AUTHOR

on the web
www.MercyBCarruthers.com

in your inbox
bit.ly/mercymafialetters

TEXT 'MERCYB' TO 555888

Made in the USA
Monee, IL
11 February 2020

21640589R00118